Welcome to Women's Group

> Meeting
> Tuesdays
> at 8:00pm
> EVERYONE IS
> WELCOME

Joyce Rebeta-Burditt

*

Joyce Rebeta-Burditt
is the author of

The Cracker Factory (Macmillan, 1977)
Triplets (Delacorte Press, 1981)
Buck Naked (Ballantine Books, 1996)

*

Dedication

Once again, for George, who laughs at my jokes
and never gave up.

The Cracker Factory 2: Welcome to Women's Group
by Joyce Rebeta-Burditt

F I R S T   E D I T I O N

ISBN: 978-1-936214-08-2
Library of Congress Control Number: 2009942291

Edited by Karen V. Kibler

Author Photo by Carol Summers

This is a work of fiction.

Special thanks to the cover models: the ladies at Mapleton Elementary School in
Oregon. Pictured clockwise from the left: Kristine Hill-Riggs, Carrie McNeill, Andrea
Milbrett, Regena Ross, Cecelia Barrett, Nikole Crabtree, MacKenzie Cleary, and Sarah
Timpe. Participated but not pictured: Debra Fleming, Laura Marshall, Janice Patterson,
Renee McCurdy, and Yvette Simington. Special thanks to Brenda Moyer, Mapleton
Elementary Administrator, and Regena Ross for coordinating the photo shoot.

Wyatt-MacKenzie Publishing, Inc.

15115 Highway 36, Deadwood, Oregon 97430
541-964-3314 ✳ www.wyattmackenzie.com

Prologue

from author Joyce Rebeta-Burditt

I'd like to welcome you to the Tuesday Night Women's Group. But first I need to tell you how I got here!

The Cracker Factory was an autobiographical novel that told my story of alcoholism and finding sobriety. In the novel, Cassie Barrett was me, and Charlie was my husband, George. My twin brother Jim was named Bobby, and my sister Mary Ann became Mary Kay.

Here's a little background, in case you haven't met Cassie yet... Cassie is a twenty-something housewife, married at eighteen, three times a mom by twenty-two. Having gone straight from her father's house yippie-skippy to her husband's house, she'd lost something in the quick daughter-to-wife transition. Herself.

Overwhelmed by her responsibilities and frightened by her increasing anger and frustration, she'd taken to sipping, then nipping from the one-drink-before-dinner scotch until occasional blackouts and empty bottles hidden in the laundry hamper finally made her admit to herself that she might have a drinking problem.

Her husband thought she was too young to have a drinking problem. All the drunks he knew were over forty. Her mother advised her to learn to drink like a lady "but don't quit because you'll be no fun at parties."

Cassie, who was becoming sicker and sicker, thought she might die from drinking before she was old enough.

With nowhere to turn, and in those days no treatment programs for alcoholism, Cassie Barrett had only one option. She signed herself into a pyschiatric ward she lovingly deemed "The Cracker Factory."

In this book, *The Cracker Factory 2: Welcome to Women's Group,* we pick up where *The Cracker Factory* left off. Cassie has embraced Alcoholics Anonymous and is a long-time member of a Women's AA Group.

Cassie and her fellow AA members help each other to live sober the lives that had become unmanageable while they were drinking. The issues they discuss—the husbands, lovers, kids, careers and emotions that sometimes threaten to go out of control—are the heartaches, triumphs and love stories shared by women everywhere, not only by those with a drinking problem.

What else, besides staying sober, has Cassie been doing for forty-plus years? I'd like to tell you that my alter ego formulated a brilliant plan and then followed it meticulously. But, I had no plan. Things happened, followed by other things, leaving me in a constant state of astonishment.

First surprise: *The Cracker Factory* became a bestseller, and it was made into an ABC-TV movie starring Natalie Wood! Then, things really started happening. The Eighties, Nineties, and up to the present have been a whirlwind of the Unplanned Life which could be subtitled "Little Alice from Cleveland Falls Down the Rabbit Hole and Lands in Wonderland (Hollywood)."

In alternating memoir chapters of *The Cracker Factory 2*, I'll take you with me through years of Hollywood life as a network executive, writer, producer, and boggle-eyed witness to celebrities, chauvinism, big producers, studios, epidemic cocaine use, and actors (both sweet and sour), all seen through my (and Cassie's) unrelentingly sober eyes.

Opposite these memoir chapters, the Women's Group invites you to sit at the table, pick up a script and play a part along with Cassie and her friends. Why stay sober? Because sober is better. Richer. More fun. Always. Relax. Listen in. The Women's Group might just help you, too.

Preface

THIS I KNOW…

In the last forty-plus years there isn't one second I've lived through, from absolute joy to utter heartbreak, that would have been made better by drinking. Not one.

Joyce Rebeta-Burditt

HEARD AND NEVER FORGOTTEN...

"Everybody's got some kind of handicap. Mine just shows."

— Kenny Veder, popping a wheelchair
wheelie in Von's parking lot ~ 1978

"Whatever works."

— Woody Allen ~ 2009

"How did I end up in rehab? I won an Oscar, for Chrissake!"

— Famous Movie Star ~ 90s

HEARD AND NEVER FORGOTTEN...

"Don't stop drinking, Honey.
You'll be no fun at parties. Just
learn to drink like a lady."
— My Mother ~ November 1967

"If I could afford Betty Ford,
I'd go there. But I can't.
And I don't have insurance,
so I can't go to one of
those thirty day programs.
That's why I like AA.
It's free. And it's like
Starbucks — there's one
on every corner. The people
there know what I'm
talking about."
— ANONYMOUS NEWBIE

Chapter 1.

Welcome to the Tuesday Women's Group of Alcoholics Anonymous. My name is Cassie and I am a recovering alcoholic. I've been in recovery, without a relapse or "slip," for forty-one years.

I hear you asking, "How did you do that?"

I can only tell you what my much loved sponsor Alice M. told me when I was a fragile and terrified newbie, awe-struck by her thirteen years of continuous sobriety. I begged her to tell me her "secret," the "magic" of long-term sobriety. "Stay sober one day at a time, Kid," Alice said. "Keep breathing in and out and pretty soon you'll be old."

I thought she was kidding. Nothing in this tangled-web world could be that simple. But as always, Alice had spoken the truth. She gave me simple directions for a complex journey, a program to follow, a new perspective and hope, all within fifteen minutes of meeting her. I followed her around like a duckling. She had the sobriety I so desperately wanted, so I hoped that by staying close, her sobriety would rub off. I soon found out that sobriety isn't like chalk. It doesn't rub off. I would actually have to work at it. This was fine with me. I knew what working hard meant. I'd already worked hard. Unfortunately up to that point, I'd worked hard only at drinking and becoming a mental patient, neither of which had been my childhood dream.

When the teacher in third grade asks the kids what they want to be when they grow up, has even one of them ever said, "I'd like to be a drunk and a demented person, please"? I think not. At least I didn't. That kid back in the corner who ate jars of paste, maybe, but definitely not me. I used to say I wanted to be a doctor, never dreaming that I would spend great chunks of my life as a patient. Right setting, wrong chair.

The second question I hear you ask is, "If you've been continually sober for forty-one years, why do you say you're still recovering?"

I'm still recovering because there's no cure for alcoholism. It's a chronic condition, like diabetes. I know people with severe diabetes and how hard they struggle to maintain their health. A friend tells me, "I'm always one chocolate binge away from a coma." That's dire. And hard. And chronic. Just like alcoholism. I can eat all the chocolate I want but I'm always one drink away from disaster.

I learned that in AA. I've learned lots in AA which is amazing, because at heart I'm a rebel and an iconoclast. I loathe rules. I loathe following the rules. I was born with an aversion to people who want to tell me what to do, even when following directions is clearly in my best interest.

I decided early in my AA life that the program would work for me. How? Instinct and logic combined. I walked into a church basement full of people who were genuinely friendly without any apparent ulterior motive, who didn't want to sell me insurance or aluminum siding or want me to bake thirty-seven PTA cupcakes by noon tomorrow, who smiled and said "welcome." Further, they told me that they were alcoholics but didn't need to drink anymore. They had no reason to lie or to be sitting in a dank, neon-lit church basement on a Saturday night if this AA thing didn't work. So I quickly decided that it worked and if it worked for them it could work for me because, much as I hated to admit it at the time, I'm no different from anyone else.

I also decided that if I heard stuff that made me roll my eyes and/or cringe, I'd ignore it. I'd just latch on to the stuff that made sense to me and not give in to one of my favorite impulses, throwing the baby out with the bathwater. In high school I'd barely listened to the brilliant lectures on Merchant of Venice given by Sister Mary Michael because she'd once said, "When girls chew gum, the Blessed Mother cries."

Cries? In Heaven? Over girls chewing gum? Were we supposed to think that the Blessed Mother has a screw loose?

I also decided that I would never, ever claim to have All, Most, Many or even Some of the answers.

We are all alcoholics here. None of us is an "expert." In particular, I am not an expert. Everything I know I've learned from other people, in and out of AA. Everything I say is my opinion, based on my personal experience and the insights I've gleaned from them.

Take from this only what makes sense to you and what you can use.

Ignore the rest.

In other words, feel free to disagree with me. Your experience isn't mine or your insights either. At my first AA meetings I made a point to look for ways in which I could relate to the speaker. Sometimes it was hard. No one can relate to everyone. But even when I couldn't relate to one moment of the speaker's experience and inwardly cringed at his/her insights, I always found that I could identify with the speaker's feelings. Every single one of us has felt fear and despair, that awful sense of impending doom, shame, depression and worst of all, the crushing isolation that comes with feeling "I am the only one who can't control my drinking." The ability to relate is all about feelings – and God do we have them. Too many, too fast, too conflicting and often, too overwhelming to bear without help. Lots of help.

But words and opinions? They are only my individual thoughts, written down. If anything helps, I'm happy. If what I say pisses you off, please forget it immediately. All I ask is that you don't throw your folding chair at me. I don't duck as fast as I used to.

Right now I'm setting up chairs for the meeting because for the next six months I'm the elected group secretary. Group secretary is the "civilian" title for Trusted Servant. All AA members get a shot at Trusted Servant. AA has no hierarchy, no officers, no dues or fees. To provide for our needs like hall rentals, coffee, chairs, cookies and newsletter printing fees among others, we pass a basket at the end of the meeting. Like the churchgoers in *Little House on the Prairie*, we dig out our change and dollar bills and toss them into the basket, passing it to our neighbor in the next chair. This way of fund-raising, obsolete everywhere except in churches and AA, is so immediate and personal that it's literally heartwarming. We take care of our own. And, more than once, I've seen a confused and ragged wretch reeking of alcohol, take a dollar or two out of the basket while everyone else looks away, thinking, "there but for the grace of God...."

Of course, if you want to send a check for megabucks to the AA Central Office in New York City, they won't tear it up. But mostly, it's passing the basket.

I'm waiting for Rachel to arrive. She's promised to come early to make the coffee. I'm not allowed to make coffee. My coffee is so bad that blue-haired Daughters of the American Revolution have been known to spit it out on damask tablecloths, then immediately expire of embarrassment. Before the invention of Prilosec, my coffee sent people to the hospital, belching fire and shrieking that their esophagus had spontaneously combusted. In the coffee pot, my brew turns mysteriously to a battery acid-like substance that eats through soft tissue and melts belt buckles. I do, however, make excellent tea.

So Rachel is coming early. In her early thirties, Rachel has been sober six years without a slip (AA-speak) or relapse (doc-speak). I like her a lot. Her current project, outside of maintaining her sobriety, is learning to express herself without swearing. I'm not sure why she wants to stop swearing. She's mastered the form. She's vivid. Inventive. Erudite. Clear. All of the best attributes of Spoken Language. She's so good she could teach swearing at UCLA Extension. But not swearing is currently important to Rachel and that's all that matters.

And here she is, five-five, curly brown hair and big warm smile:

Rachel

Hey!

Cassie

Hey! How's it going?

Rachel

I'm still sober and I haven' fu…oops…killed anyone today.

I give her a thumbs up.

Cassie

Great! You're practically a saint.

Rachel goes off to make coffee and I wave at Leslie and Katherine who are walking in together. Leslie is a tall, slim, twenty-something blonde lawyer who's been sober six months. She's so elegantly and perfectly attractive that the unevolved women among us (me) must fight an occasional impulse to surround her and pelt her with pasta fazool. Of course we would never, ever do that, honest. Leslie's a newbie and fragile. Maybe in ten, fifteen years, we'll pelt her. Or maybe we'll have conquered our (my) childish envy of unattainable perfection in others.

Katherine isn't so much walking as shuffling and pushing her walker. She's seventy-two and has been sober for two and a half years. I pay close attention when she talks because there's nothing I admire as much as courage and Katherine is brave.

Now we're joined at the table by Terri, who's either seventeen or eighteen depending on her mood. She shows up almost every week but hangs back, like a dog circling the campfire, wary and surly but hungry for scraps. She's been showing up for about four months, often refuses to talk and is invariably withdrawn. None of us knows anything about her or if she's clean and sober or why she comes. Obviously our Tuesday night meeting is a safe place for her. We do our best to make her feel welcome, knowing that because she keeps coming back, she's getting something from the meetings even though we aren't sure what. If it's only consistency, that's a lot. No matter what chaos is going on in this girl's life, she knows that every Tuesday night at eight, the meeting will be here for her.

Terri is followed by Elena who, as usual, is carrying her baby, Lucy. Usually kids aren't allowed at AA meetings because they don't need to hear what we talk about, but Elena is nursing and her husband works nights so when she first showed up with newborn Lucy and said she needed to be here, what could we do? For now we're pretending that Lucy is invisible and hoping a solution will present itself which we expect will happen.

Rachel arrives with a cup of coffee which she places before Katherine.

Rachel

(to Katherine)

Three sugars.

(to everyone)

Coffee's ready.

Katherine

(to Rachel)

Thanks, Sweetie.

Everyone goes off to get coffee, then returns. I get down to business. The meeting begins.

On most Tuesday nights we're a small group so I don't ask in advance who wants to read what. I just assume that we're all willing to read anything at all, so I just hand the material around the table.

Leslie reads the Twelve Steps, Katherine reads the Twelve Traditions, Rachel reads Chapter Five from the Big Book, *How It Works,* and then I make a few general announcements.

Cassie

Every week in this hall there are sixteen AA meetings including two women's and a men's. We're lucky. We have our own hall. All AA, all the time. We're right here. You can't miss us. We're at the end of that Yellow Brick Road you've been traveling.

Arbitrarily, I start with Rachel.

Cassie

Rachel?

Rachel

Well, this has been one shi…oops…crazy week. The kids were all sick, one after the other with a virus they brought home from school. I thought it was strep so I took them for throat swabs but it was just sore throats and you know that my mother-in-law's always saying that I'm overprotective because of all those years I was lying around shit-faced ignoring the kids…oh my God, I said shit-faced, crap, I owe myself two dollars for that and two for crap.

Anyway, maybe my mother-in-law's right. Where would my kids be if she hadn't been there while I was drinking? Nowhere, that's where. So if I still have a little tiny resentment that my mother-in-law still thinks she's my kids' mom and I'm just some visiting nitwit who could go off the God...gosh darned deep end any second, I should get over it. Right? I mean she was so good to me and my kids and my husband, Stan. When I was all passed out on cheap wine she was the one in the kitchen making pot roast. Still is.

Stan loves her pot roast. She makes it with noodles. I used to make it with potatoes but the noodles are great. Her gravy's better than mine, too. Everybody says so. And she loves babysitting. She said she wouldn't mind if I came to a meeting every night of the week. She and Stan like the same TV shows so when I'm out they watch TV together.

Ya know, I'm one of those gals who didn't drink over the big things. When my mom was sick I took care of her. When she died, I arranged everything. It was the little things, like the sink stopping up that sent me running for the bottle. So with Evelyn taking care of most of that stuff...well maybe that's a good thing, ya think?

(pause)

That's all.

Cassie

Thank you for sharing. Terri?

Terri

Hi, I'm Terri and I'm an ungrateful alcoholic
and I don't know why I keep coming back
here. For me staying clean and sober doesn't
feel much better than not being clean and
sober. It's all one big gray blob. Either way, all
I really want to do is stay in bed, eat potato
chips and watch TV. For sure I'm going to lose
my job. Who cares? I've worked at half the
dry cleaners in town. I can work at the other
half. And in case you're wondering, I don't
like any of you.

Cassie

That's okay, Terri. We're glad you're here.

    (then)

Katherine?

Katherine

I'm Katherine and I'm a grateful alcoholic but
I sure can identify with Terri. Days when I
wake up with every joint throbbin' and feelin'
like someone's rubbin' ground glass into 'em,
I'd just as soon shoot folks as look at 'em. I'll
tell you, I wake up a bitch. Takes four Advil
and three cups of coffee before I feel like I
might want to live another day.

But I said I'm grateful and I am. I'm grateful
that I outlived my husband. 'Course he was
twenty years older'n me so that wasn't hard.
The hard part was that we weren't friends and
forget lovers after the first coupla years – we
was drinking buddies. Hard drinking buddies.
Fighting all the time. What do you call

that…sparring partners. Actual fistfights. Oh, it was grim. Awful. For years and years we went to work and came home and drank and fought until he retired and then I retired and then it was just boozing and fighting until he got sick and got DTs and went to the hospital and died.

Then I got sick and they took me to the hospital and a lady from AA came to see me and asked if I'd like to get sober and I said God, yes or I'm better off dead. So I went to a halfway house where they took care of me and I got sober. Funny thing was while I was drinkin' I didn't know I had arthritis but when I stopped it hit like a hammer. But I made up my mind I'm not dyin' like the old man no matter what. I'm dyin' sober, not rantin' and ravin' and that's that.

(pause)

My mornin's are hell but by noon I can smile and come evenin' I'm here with you all. And nobody ever turns me down when I ask for a ride. You are all God's angels.

Cassie

Thank you, Katherine. Leslie?

Leslie

I'm Leslie and I'm a recovering alcoholic. I am so very pleased that I could be here tonight. I am so very grateful for every second of my six months of sobriety. I'm grateful to AA and to each of you, I had no idea what to do and you told me. Your direction and encouragement have been crucial to my success. I haven't finished reading the Big Book yet but I will.

(smiles)

I love that it's quaint, like an historical novel.
People back then were…um…fervent…
weren't they? Not that we aren't today.

(quickly)

I'll finish reading the book.

(pause)

I know I don't have the serious problems that
many of you have. I'm not dealing with finan-
cial or relationship issues. I'm not yet married
and I don't have children. I'm very grateful
that when I do have a family I'll be sober so I
won't make catastrophic mistakes.

(smiles)

I almost didn't make it to the meeting tonight.
I have a case that could use more research.

(little laugh)

But then what case couldn't? I mean, when
you get to court you want everything to be
perfect, right? Especially when you're a
woman. The other women in the firm, the
older women, tell me it's better than it used to
be, but it's still a boys' club, you know? The
ceiling got cracked like Hillary said but it's not
broken yet, so if you work with men you've
got to figure a way to present yourself as one
of the boys but subtly, not in their faces.

For example, the guys can get falling down
drunk but a woman's got to watch it because
falling down drunk in a guy is "boys will be
boys" but in a woman it's ugly. We all know
that men don't like "ugly" in women. And

when the guys talk about how they manipulate their wives or girlfriends or both of them,
you can't ever take the woman's side. You just
say things like "I hear you." You have to
pretend that you think like they do, that most
of the time women just aren't worth the
trouble.

(looking around)

It was you women who taught me that no
matter the situation, I didn't have to drink.
You told me it was the first drink that got me
drunk. You told me to think that first drink
through. You told me that if I didn't drink, if I
called one of you or went to a meeting
instead, the Moment would pass and the solution would come.

(smiling)

You were right. Socializing is a big part of my
business. The other night I was out with an
important client. I could see that he was
wondering why I was drinking ginger ale. He
asked if I wasn't feeling well. I told him I was
feeling fine. He looked uncomfortable, then
actually edgy. He was scowling at me, fiddling
with his glass. I could hear him tapping his
foot. I got worried. If you make your client
uncomfortable, he goes somewhere else. I
mean, it's his money. So, I thought maybe I
should order a drink. Just hold it, not drink it.
Then I thought, no that's stupid, he'd notice
that, too. I couldn't call any of you with him
sitting there. But then, all of a sudden, I got an
idea. I invited him back to my place where I
screwed his brains out. He's one happy client
and I didn't drink. So, thank you, Ladies,
thank you. That's it.

The women around the table, including me, stared at Leslie. No one said anything. Sharing is not a conversation, open for comment. It's the individual's Moment to speak his/her mind without fear of judgment. Occasionally one of us forgets that.

Katherine

Don't thank us for that! Nobody told you to act like a damn floozie!

Cassie

No cross talk, please Katherine! Elena?

Elena

Hi. I'm Elena and I'm an alcoholic. I didn't even think about drinking this week even though I got hardly any sleep. Lucy's got her days and nights turned around again so she's up all night and sleeps most of the day. Sometimes between three and four AM when I'm dead on my feet and she's screaming, I get this gosh-awful craving but I know it's for sleep and not for a drink so I just ignore it.

Funny how the mind lies to you. When I was a kid, a nun gave me a holy picture of Satan dressed up like a gorgeous angel whispering temptations in a little girl's ear. She said Satan was like that, a beautiful liar. Since I've been sober that's how I see booze. Promises heaven and gives you hell.

So right now I'm just putting one foot in front of other and doing my best and here I am tonight with you guys, thank you God. And I am, really, really grateful. That's all.

Cassie

Thank you, Elena. Has anyone heard from Christa?

Rachel

I got an email from her. Christa and her mom are doing that big antique drive that runs through five or six states in the Midwest. They're going to hit AA meetings along the way. She says she'll bring back pictures.

Cassie

Great.

(then)

Okay, my turn.

(then)

You guys know me. I can tell you I've been sober today and this evening and I've had a lot of days when I could say that. You know that they've happened one day at a time. When I was new, my days happened one hour at a time or ten minutes at a time, and sometimes, crying and terrified, seconds at a time.

When I was new, I walked into my first meeting in a Parma Heights, Ohio, church basement. I stood in the doorway looking confused and not knowing what to do. A short, bald fifty-something man walked up and asked if he could help me. I told him I was looking for an AA meeting, that I was an alcoholic.

He stared, then laughed incredulously, "You!

You're a kid!" Faster than lightening, a blonde
woman his age swooped up behind him,
thumped him on the shoulder and said, "If
she says she's an alcoholic, she's an alcoholic."
Then she held out her hand to me. "I'm Alice
and this moron is my husband, John. We're
both alcoholics. Come sit with me."

(then)

She taught me everything I know. She taught
me that alcoholism is a disease of mind and
body. No cure but that I could stop suffering
from its effects. I could follow the AA
program, created in 1935 by two alcoholics,
the visionary Bill Wilson and his first convert,
Dr. Bob Smith, neither of whom could stay
sober until Bill Wilson was struck with the
amazing insight that by helping others get
sober he might stay sober himself. It worked.

(then)

Alice taught me that I drank about my feelings. If I was sad or angry I drank. If I was
happy or elated I drank. If I was cranky or
mean or loving and sweet…you get the idea.
Alice told me that when she got sober she
tried not to have any feelings at all, thinking
that not having feelings would be easier. She
found out that feelings aren't optional. We all
got 'em. We have to learn to live with them
sober.

(then)

Gosh, it's getting late. No souls saved after ten
o'clock. I'll wrap this up. Alice told me to sit
down, shut up and listen. She told me to suit
up and show up at meetings. She told me to
find a sponsor so that an idiot wouldn't be

running my life. She was my sponsor, my friend and my Warrior Woman. She taught me how to save my own life.

(then)

Here's the basket.

We passed the basket, then I read *A Vision For You*. I always read *A Vision For You* when I'm Trusted Servant because I'm selfish and it's the loveliest essay of written encouragement I've ever read and I love to read it aloud. Then we stood and joined hands and said the Serenity Prayer, ending with "Keep Coming Back! It Works If You Work It!" And the meeting was over.

I asked Terri if she'd clean out the coffee pot and Leslie if she'd help with the chairs. They both said yes.

I folded two chairs and carried them to the corner where Leslie was stacking two more on a pile of twenty. Leslie was scowling.

"Who the hell does Katherine think she is?" Leslie asked me. "She's not supposed to judge."

"She's not judging you, Leslie. She's <u>telling</u> you, in her own politically incorrect way, that she's worried about you. So am I."

"Because I slept with a guy?" Her eyes narrowed. "You...older...women think that nobody should have sex. You didn't have it so nobody should."

I laughed. "Are you kidding, Leslie? We didn't have sex? You're talking about the late Sixties and Seventies. You're talking about the Pill and the Summer of Love. You're talking about sex without worrying about AIDS. If you wanted sex, it was free and there was nothing to stop you. That's why your grandma calls it the good old days."

"Then why is Katherine mad at me?"

"She's not mad. She's grumpy. Every joint in her body's on fire, so everything she says comes out grouchy. I don't know how she gets through the day but she does. The reason that Katherine and I are concerned is that your…um…wham-bam with your colleague wasn't about sex. If you liked him or loved him or even thought he was hot, then *that* would have been sex. But you were just trying to play him. You were trying to make yourself comfortable by using sex the same way you used drinking. You're just substituting one self-destructive behavior for the other."

"Having sex with a guy is no big deal," Leslie said.

"Sometimes it isn't," I agreed. "But when your reason for having sex is the same reason you had for drinking, shouldn't you start wondering what you're doing?"

She shot me a look of pure defiance. "When you sleep with guys right away, they don't hurt you."

So, here it was, the Heart of the Matter. "Someone hurt you, Leslie?" I said softly.

I waited. Her face shadowed. She looked away. She held her breath. She was trying to decide between spilling it all out whatever it was, and risk falling apart, or holding it all in as she had for far too long. She glared at me. "I never said that anyone hurt me. I have to go. I have an early meeting."

Leslie grabbed her purse from the table and headed for the door. I followed her. "I'll be here tomorrow night for the Speaker Meeting. Come fifteen minutes early and we'll talk. Okay?"

Leslie didn't answer. She kept going. I sighed and went into the back room looking for Terri. I found the coffee urn, sparkling clean and dry but Terri was gone, like vapor drifting off into the night. Likely, she'd tiptoed out the door when I was talking to Leslie, thinking I'd asked her to stay because I wanted to "talk."

What I wanted to do was listen. I've seen so often what can happen when a withdrawn person finally talks. The floodgates open, the crap pours out, the armor falls off and the real person appears without what we call "the wreckage of our past." This wreckage, the mistakes we made while we were drinking and the guilt associated with them are like the chains worn by Marley's ghost, perpetually dragging us backwards into the hell of our past unless we drop them. We AAs have been down these roads and through these swamps. We know where the booby traps are hidden and where the sinkholes wait. We know where the snakes live. We know the pitfalls that we've encountered and avoided, and the obstacles others have shared. This knowledge is all we have to pass on. That it's enough to help another human being establish sobriety, is the miracle of AA. It's enough and it works.

We can't change the past, ever. I'd give a lot if I could change certain things in my past. But I can't. And I can't drag the past along with me either. The mistakes of the past are too heavy a burden to place on even the sturdiest sobriety. And sobriety is everything. The past is the door we've stepped through. Tomorrow is the door we have yet to open. We have only today to make our amends as best we can to the people we've hurt. And to not take that first drink.

Turning off the lights, it occurs to me that I need to find a meeting for Terri that has more people her own age. Alcoholic teens who are in recovery aren't as rare as they used to be. Terri might do well in a group where she isn't the only kid with metallic green nail polish, and who is texting and tweeting before and after meetings. Terri will always be welcome here but she needs her peers, too, just like the rest of us.

I do not sponsor either Terri or Leslie. They haven't asked me. If one of them does, I'll explain that I sponsor by Alice's Rules, the way she sponsored me. If they run away screaming, I'll understand. Alice was tough. She was demanding. Sometimes she could be downright aggravating. On one memorable occasion I found myself wishing that Scottie would beam her up. In my second year of sobriety, Alice sent me to speak at the Midnight Mission downtown. I found myself dressed in a circle skirt, sweater and loafers – the very young Mrs. Dimples from the suburbs telling my "life story" to a roomful of grizzled, homeless men who had to listen to me before they got any supper. The few who looked me in the eye did so balefully or with open hostility. I choked on every third word. Who was I to tell these men (and back then it was all men) how to find sobriety?

What hubris! What nerve! What raging gall! I'd experienced none of what they'd experienced. Most of them were middle-aged or older but a few were veterans just back from Vietnam, shell-shocked (PTSD was not a term in use then), generally scorned and addicted. The men in that room were fighting demons I couldn't even imagine. I had nothing to offer them but an account of twelve years of Catholic school and life in the suburbs and the idea that our common disease of alcoholism made me one of them. So that's what I told them, then apologized for being there, and I think for living, and slunk out of the Mission early so they could eat.

At home I called Alice after nine PM (against Alice's Rules) and told her that I felt completely flattened and humbled by the pain I'd seen and felt in these men. She said, "Good. Don't forget it." Then she hung up on me.

Alice called Sponsorship, The Great Dilemma. "To be or not to be a sponsor." If we choose to be sponsors, we have to remember that we're not doctors or experts. We're alcoholics, hopefully with the lengthy and solid sobriety that qualifies us as AA tour guides.

But when we sponsor and give it our all and the person we're sponsoring goes back out and gets drunk and crazy and locked up and dead, it breaks our hearts. We know that we didn't make them alcoholics and can't make them sober, but damn, it hurts. And you bet we cry. Some people sponsor all the time. It's truly their calling. They are *great* sponsors and should go about wearing halos of light so that everyone can know them for the angels they are. I don't know how they do it. I truly don't. But I bow deeply.

Right now I need to put the basket money in the locked drawer and go home to my husband who worries if I'm not home before the eleven o'clock news. You'd like him. He's funny. He's also a former Marine and present golfer and the very grateful spouse of a recovering alcoholic.

C H A P T E R   T W O

HAVING LONG-TERM SOBRIETY IS LIKE WINNING AN ACADEMY Award. There are so many people to thank that you just get started when the music comes up and they yank you off the stage with a giant hook.

I have people to thank, literally hundreds, maybe thousands of people, from the psychiatrist who put me in a safe place, a psychiatric hospital, to a man I heard at a meeting on a night I was in personal turmoil. He said, "Serenity is when you're dead. That's okay, I'll stay sober anyway." I never knew your name Sir, but thank you, thank you. You reminded me that staying sober has nothing to do with feelings, just when I needed to be reminded. Feelings come and go, the good and the bad. Sobriety stays, holding us steady when those feelings threaten to blow us over. As we remain sober, we find it easier and easier to not act on feelings that once literally drove us crazy, easier and easier to take a deep breath and "decide" rather than have our feelings decide for us.

We have only one decision to make every day, only one. That decision is not to drink.

That decision becomes easier and easier, too, until I promise you, it's no longer a decision but second nature.

"I don't drink" hasn't been a daily battle for me for so long, I can't remember when I stopped waking up in the morning afraid that I might not get through the day, shaking with anxiety and reaching for the Big Book, my lifeline, to read a couple of pages before I dared get out of bed. I can't remember when I had my last "drunk dream," those dreams of drinking so vivid, I woke up thinking I'd actually gone out and had a drink. I'd wake from those dreams sweating and so disappointed in myself that I'd blown my sobriety, I'd literally want to die. Then I'd realize it was a dream and wonder what I was doing wrong that I should have such a nightmare. I didn't know then that "drunk dreams" are just a normal, if terrifying, part of getting sober, a symptom of the disease. I always took them as a sign that I needed to work harder on my sobriety, not a bad thing.

Some people I've known have assumed that I've never had a slip because I grasped the program so firmly or with some special insight. Not true. The truth is that I'm a craven coward. I've never understood why I was given that one stunning Moment of Grace when all my defenses came crashing down and I knew in my soul that I was an alcoholic and couldn't get well alone. I only know that the sense of freedom that followed, the "click" of being in the right place at the right time and on the right path was an experience that took me out of myself. I didn't ask for this experience. I didn't deserve it or at least not more than any other alcoholic muddling around in the quagmire that's alcoholism. I hadn't DONE anything to deserve it. There wasn't and isn't anything special about me. Yet, this experience was GIVEN to me. I didn't understand it then. I don't understand it now.

I understand that many people, over time, have had such experiences and talked about them, thanking the Higher Power of their belief. The part I don't understand is, why me?

I'm hardly the type of believer any traditional Higher Power would point to with pride. A very kind Higher Power would call me a "work in progress" with the emphasis on "work" and "progress" a matter of opinion. And yet, I was given this remarkable experience free of charge and with no strings attached. Since I don't understand the "why me" of it, I would have to be incredibly stupid not to be profoundly grateful forever. I can't and don't expect another experience like this. Ever. If I was to waste it by drinking again, I deserve to have lightening strike me. I always knew in my heart that if I allowed myself just one slip, I'd never get back to sobriety. I still know it. That knowledge helps me stay sober. Of all the things I don't know, I **do** know that you don't mess with a Universe that gives you extraordinary gifts.

That gift was given to me while I was sitting on a metal stool in a storage room in the psychiatric ward of a general hospital. I was in the storage room because that morning, all of the interview rooms (the rooms where shrinks and their patients stare at each other, each hoping that the other will say something rational) were full and my shrink couldn't wait for a room to open. He was the president of the Ohio APA and had to preside over one of those meetings where shrinks discuss patients in technical terms (she's mad as a hatter) and eat chocolate cake.

He'd just left the room after telling me, "I don't know what else to do with you. Call AA or somethin'."

Then, bang, he was out the door, leaving me furious. HE didn't know what to do with me? I PAID him to know what to do with me. If he didn't know what to do with me, what the hell could I do with me?

As I sat in the silence, surrounded by mops, brooms and buckets, IT happened. Just like that. The Experience. Like sunlight entering my heart, the burden lifted, gone, vanished out the barred window, leaving me lighter than air and stunned with wonder.

Just like that.

To the therapeutic community: yes, I know, my doctor had skillfully brought me to the brink, then abandoned me at just the right Moment, leaving me to sit with myself and my problem. It took me two days to tell him I'd had a conversion experience because "stunned with wonder" means just that. For two days I felt I dare not speak of it. I was afraid that the feeling would go away. When I did tell him he was very excited. He actually laughed and clapped his hands, looking so pleased with both of us that I had to laugh, too. When I told him that I'd actually called AA and made contact and that an AA "lady" was coming to see me, he gave me a thumbs up. In that Moment in that room, the therapeutic process had produced a healing breakthrough and we both felt its power.

I make fun of shrinks because, let's face it, it's easy. Outside of lawyers, shrinks are prime joke material and even easier than lawyers because their ways are so mysterious to laymen and their foibles are ripe for the plucking.

And yet I know better than anyone that good psychiatrists, psychologists, and psychiatric nurses have saved and are saving many of our lives, pointing us in the right direction and encouraging and supporting us on our journey. Without their guidance and support, many of us, including myself, would have stumbled and fallen, either by drinking again or becoming overwhelmed by the anxiety and depression that is so often a part of the disease of alcoholism.

In the Big Book of AA, we read, "There are those, too, who suffer from grave emotional and mental disorders, but many of them do recover if they have the capacity to be honest."

I've always been impressed that, way back in the 30s, the founders, Bill Wilson and Dr. Bob Smith knew enough to recognize that separate mental and emotional problems could make the attainment of sobriety much more difficult. Back then, little was generally known about the treatment of mental and emotional problems. The usual treatment for mental disorders, institutionalization, only warehoused people without curing them or offering treatment that allowed them to maintain themselves independently.

In my own family, a bright and creative aunt graduated from "nervous wreck" (first diagnosis by an MD) while she was ranting about government conspiracies to "mental patient" when she set fire to the attic. Institutionalized on and off for years, she mysteriously got better (100% rational) at the age of sixty. As "mental patient," her diagnosis was schizoid personality. She told me later that everyone she met in "that place" was diagnosed with schizoid personality from the homicidal to the catatonic. The thirties were a long time ago....

As I said at the beginning, everything I say is only my opinion and I know that some will disagree with me, but it is my deeply held belief that mental disorders can't be resolved only by staying sober and working the program. There are those among us who need more help. We wouldn't expect sobriety to enable a person with a broken leg to run a marathon. We can't expect sobriety and even a program as effective as AA to mend a broken mind. It's not fair to the troubled person to expect him/her to maintain sobriety without appropriate help.

Ideally, this appropriate help would involve therapy and often involve medication. Since we now know that many mental problems have as their underlying cause an imbalanced brain chemistry, and medications to balance that brain chemistry are now available, it would be cruel to deny a recovering alcoholic either therapy or medication, either by lack of information or the misguided opinion that the program solves all.

I don't pretend to have medical expertise. I have none. But I have had the benefit of therapists without whom I might have ended my life sober or engaged in other self-destruction, again stone-cold sober. I thank them and bless them for their support and am grateful they were there when I needed them.

Also, in forty-one years of sobriety, I have seen people who were clearly mentally ill come into AA, and struggle valiantly to grasp at sobriety only to be defeated by their mental illnesses. I've seen the bag ladies and homeless men sitting in the back, muttering to themselves, holding themselves and rocking; the apparently well, the mom with untreated depression, the man with untreated bipolar disorder, "sponsoring" one day, weeping the next. I was there in the AA hall when a man named Ray started telling his sponsor that he was hearing voices that told him to kill his wife. He knew the voices were wrong but he couldn't make them stop. Ray's sponsor took him to County General where they held him for seventy-two hours but released him without follow-up and only twenty anti-psychotic pills. When the voices came back, Ray's sponsor took him to the police station where Ray begged them to lock him up. The police said they couldn't. He hadn't committed a crime.

Ray killed his wife with a shotgun and her father, too. When he came up for sentencing, the judge asked him if there was anything he wanted to say. He said, "Yes. Don't ever let me out."

We cried for his wife and her father. We cried for Ray. We cursed a system that can't or won't help the untreated mentally ill or has no idea how to do it. The system is wrong. It doesn't work. If we as a people had better priorities, we'd fix it. Until we do, nothing good will happen for the untreated mentally ill or the people who live with them.

In AA, each of us knows someone or several someones struggling with mental illness. Those fortunate enough to find the outside help they need "to grasp and maintain sobriety" do very well. Those who don't, come and go or just go and God knows what happens to them.

Alcoholism is a disease. Diabetes is a disease. Mental illness is a disease. Pneumonia is a disease. Shame shouldn't be part of any of them. We're all human beings. We get sick. When we get sick we're entitled to the best help we can get, whatever the illness. If you're sick, get help. You're not alone and you don't have to feel this way.

Like diabetes, alcoholism and even mental illness are diseases that can be maintained. These diseases aren't a matter of "fault." Recovery is another matter. Recovery from a maintainable illness is the sole responsibility of the patient. If you're diabetic and know it and continue to eat sugar and fat and never exercise, it's foolish to wonder why your disease gets worse, why your vision is dimming and people you don't know want to hack off your leg. You're doing it to yourself, buddy. Harsh but true. You've been told what to do to recover....

The same is true of alcoholism and mental illness, with mental illness owning the caveat of diminished responsibility just because the system that's supposed to help is so shoddy and refusing help is so often a symptom of mental illness. If you're alcoholic and you've been told what to do and taken by the hand and shown what to do and you don't do it and your life turns to crap, don't come crying. You were told what would happen if you drank again. Just please, please come back, grab the AA program and its people and hang on. This time do it right. Maintain.

If you're mentally ill, please search for help if you can or ask someone you trust to assist you. This is a road no one can walk down alone. If you feel you're too depressed to even ask for help, make one little phone call to any mental health facility listed in the Yellow Pages. You can make that call lying in bed. You don't have to get up or wash your face. Just lie there, but call. I know it's hard and you're so very tired. But you can do it. Then let the help happen. Accept it. Don't "yes, but…" the would-be helper with objections and conditions, like "I can't" or "maybe tomorrow." You CAN do it now. I know you can. Been there. Done that. So can you.

So you've tried AA and are convinced that it won't work for you? Try something else. There are programs everywhere, all kinds of programs from faith-based to rigorously secular. Call the Alcoholism Council. Talk to a Human Resources counselor at work, at the senior center, at church, at your local hospital. Keep looking until you find the program that fits you. If you say you want help but can't find a program that fits, then you don't want to stop drinking. Nothing is perfect, not AA, not any other program. And even if there was such a thing, trust me, we alcoholics would find fault with it anyway. When we truly want to stop drinking we no longer look for "perfect." We look for sobriety.

On the other side of sloggy, suck-hole depression is LIFE, the life we are meant to have. If our brain chemistry is whacked, by a little or a lot, we have a right to correct it if we can. We have a right for ourselves and an obligation to those with whom we share our lives. Our faulty brain chemistry is like a dead squirrel under the house. Eventually the odor spreads and drives everyone crazy. We need to bury that squirrel so everyone can breathe.

Back in the day when I sobered up, there weren't any alcoholism treatment programs. The programs didn't come into being until the AMA decided that alcoholism was a disease and not a character disorder. Once alcoholism was deemed a disease, programs could be established. Insurance companies could then establish the category of "substance abuse treatment" which paid for part or all of most programs excepting the very high end, allowing many more people to get help.

But back then, no programs. Most alcoholics, particularly women, lived out their disease to its inevitable end: they died, went crazy, ended up on the streets, were committed to state institutions. I was lucky. I had the means that allowed me to see a psychiatrist. My leap into therapy began in a strange way. One afternoon in my kitchen, I was reaching for a bottle of scotch when I was overwhelmed by a feeling that something was terribly wrong. It was two in the afternoon and I was going to have a drink "to relax." I knew from experience that likely I'd have another after that and then maybe another or maybe I'd wait and have my "official" drink after my husband came home from work.

I began to wonder. Is this normal? And, yes, I was that naïve.

I called the family internist. When his receptionist put him through, he asked what was wrong. I said, "I think I have a drinking problem." I held my breath.

"Oh, really?" he said.

"Yes." I was still holding my breath, turning blue.

After hemming and hawing a bit, he told me that he didn't treat "those kinds of Problems" but he could refer me to several psychiatrists who might help.

I called the first on the list he gave me because it was the only name I could remember. When I told my husband I wanted to see a shrink, he said, "Okay, if that's what you want." Apparently he knew me better than I thought he did.

At my first session with the only shrink whose name I could remember, I was dismayed that he was so young, only five years older than I. Since I was in my early twenties, his youth unnerved me. In a shrink as in an airline pilot, a little gray hair is reassuring. He asked me why I was there.

"I think I have a drinking problem," I said, then held my breath.

He asked me my age, how often I drank and how much I drank and advised me to breathe. I answered his questions and breathed. He stared at me.

"You're depressed and anxious," he announced.

Evidently by the criteria in those days, I was too young and didn't drink enough to have a "drinking problem." These days we know better. Pre-teens and teens are welcomed into programs every day to get clean and sober.

Three years after my initial session, my shrink had learned more about alcoholism and of course, my disease had progressed. I drank too much often enough to fit the most stringent standards of alcoholism. I was completely out of control and suicidal.

Success at last!

I say I was lucky because my stay in the psychiatric ward lasted nearly three months. After three weeks, I was allowed to go to AA meetings which were held at regular groups outside the hospital. At that time, there were no in-hospital meetings so I was given "passes" to go out. When I'd return from a meeting, there was always a nurse there to greet me, ask me how the meeting went and smell my breath.

In order to attend meetings, I was given permission to use my car, which meant that I had a once-a-week pass to go home and spend an afternoon with my kids who were as confused as I was. It didn't help that my mother, humiliated by my disease, had told the kids that I was in the hospital with a gallbladder problem. Even after I told the kids the truth, they had to sit in church every Sunday while the priest, at the behest of my mom, asked the congregation to pray for a cure for my "gallbladder" (I could hear people I knew in the congregation, "Why don't they take her damn gallbladder out, for God's sake?").

I wrote about my stay in the psychiatric ward in a book called The Cracker Factory, which to myself I always called, "The Dingbat's Guide to the Loonie Bin." What might seem to some an uncomfortable experience was for me, the turning point in my life. I met myself there, got sober and grew up. And got to watch

Dark Shadows every day at three.

One of my ever-evolving beliefs is that getting sober takes more than thirty days. At my thirty-day mark, my body may have been sober (sort of) but my head was still a woozy, wobbly mess. I'm convinced that for some or maybe all of us, the kind of full sobriety that means we have both feet on the ground and can trust our own judgment with some consistency, takes much longer than thirty days. Until we have that full sobriety, we can be like leaves in the wind, blown this way and that by the smallest breeze. In a perfect world, substance abuse programs would be a minimum of sixty days with ninety the optimum. I know that this is cost-prohibitive, but the number of alcoholics able to maintain long-term sobriety would increase dramatically with more time in programs. This is not only my experience but also the experience of other people who've been fortunate enough to have extended time in treatment. It's not a guarantee but it definitely helps.

In those early days, with my hospital passes and Woody station wagon, I tried to find meetings close to the hospital. Because the hospital was on the East Side of Cleveland and I was born and raised on the West Side, to me Cleveland was like two distinct cities.

Back then there were West Side folks who'd never been East and the reverse, no kidding. The prevailing Eastsider position was that the East had the culture and the West the kielbasa while the Westsiders opined that in a downpour, the Eastsiders would drown like turkeys because they walked around with their noses stuck up to the air. Both opinions were just a tad biased.

But for me at that time, driving around the East Side at night was like driving through a foreign country. I didn't know where I was going or even where I'd been. On top of that, I was chronically confused, rolling down unfamiliar streets guided only by my woozy, wobbly head and the conviction that I was trying to do the right thing. This conviction was so strong that I actually felt that I was being protected against all evil and accident by my very own guardian angels. No matter what, no harm could come to me. Obviously, I should have not been allowed out without a keeper but sometimes delusions are helpful and this one kept me from freaking out when I got lost. I got lost a lot.

One night I'd been driving in circles for more than an hour without finding a street that I knew led back to the hospital. The streets I was driving down were looking scarier and scarier. The East Side, like the West Side, wasn't all green grass and roses hedges. There were neighborhoods where you went at your own risk and this was one of them. I turned down a narrow street lined on both sides with bars and derelict buildings. Suddenly, just ahead, I saw my salvation: two police cars, lights flashing, double parked in front of a bar. I pulled up behind one of the police cars, jumped out of my Woody and ran into the bar. Inside there seemed to have been some sort of brawl. Men, some of them bloody, all of them swearing, were lined against a wall. Four police officers, guns drawn, were telling them to shut up. A man, bloodier than the others, lay sprawled on the floor but was breathing. I went to the closest police officer and tugged on his sleeve. He whirled around, stared, said, "What the hell…!"

"Excuse me," I said, "I'm a patient at St. Luke's. I have a pass to go out to an AA meeting but I got lost coming back and I can't find the hospital. Can you help me, please?"

The officer asked, "You're a what, where?"

I repeated my story. He asked, "What kind of patient?"

"Psychiatric," I said.

"Jeez." He motioned to another officer who came over. My story was repeated. The officers conferred, quickly deciding that I was a nutcase escaped from the nut-ward and they'd better get me back in a hurry. In low, soothing tones they explained that one officer would drive my car while I would ride with the other officer, wouldn't that be nice?

I'd only asked for directions but once again, here were my angels taking care of me. I was so tired and confused from riding in circles that I was happy to let the nice policemen take me "home."

The officer who drove me didn't talk, just glanced at me

warily from time to time. I was interested to hear on the police radio that the bleeding man on the bar floor had been transported to the hospital.

My officer pulled up to St. Luke's Emergency entrance, jumped out of the car and went in. As he exited the car, I heard the doors automatically lock. How nice, I thought. He wants to make certain I'm safe. I could see the Officer talking to an orderly behind the desk, then speaking on a hospital phone. After a few moments he came out and opened the car door.

"Yeah, I guess you belong here. They said they've been waiting for you."

He escorted me to the door, where the second Officer handed me my car keys. "You're parked in C-11," he said. "Get a map at a gas station."

I thanked them profusely. They'd been so nice. I waved goodbye. They waved back.

The man at the desk showed me the path to the elevator. I punched the button for the Seventh Floor. I emerged on the Seventh Floor feeling like the whole evening had been a great success. The meeting had been an inspiration. Getting lost could have been much worse. After all, I'd gotten help before I ran out of gas. And I'd discovered that the Cleveland PD does indeed Protect and Serve. What could be better?

A nurse buzzed me in through the locked door. My shrink was in the hall waiting for me. At the time, I was so confused it didn't occur to me that it was now after midnight, not exactly his usual visiting time. It didn't occur to me that the hospital had called him when I didn't show up and he'd come over. It didn't occur to me that he'd been worried about me. I don't refer to myself as a dingbat for nothing.

"What happened?" he asked.

I told him about getting lost, the double parked police cars, the bleeding man on the floor, the escort back to the hospital. His expression never changed. Finally he nodded. "I'll bring you a map from a gas station."

Chapter 3.

The meeting's been underway for a few minutes.
Happy as I am to see that Leslie came back, I'm worried because
Terri is a no-show.

Elena

I know I shouldn't complain, but I'm starting
to feel like a single mom. I shouldn't complain
because Rick works hard all night and takes
care of Lucy all day, but he told me he goes
out to breakfast with his buds at the end of his
shift and. . .

(deep breath)

I don't go nowhere at the end of my shift. I go
home. I don't go eat with friends.

(sigh)

I don't have friends. I have a resentment.

(sniffling)

I'm a terrible person.

Cassie

No, you're not. You're young and exhausted.

(then)

We're your friends. Have a cookie.

Rachel?

Rachel

I'm not supposed to hang on to resentments so I'm getting this off of my chest. If I was drinking again I'd kill Stan. I might kill him anyway without friggin' drinking.

(then)

He's been on me for slacking off, can you believe that? A goddamn slacker. Oh forget the no swearing thing… It's the only goddamn thing I do to blow off steam. I'm no freaking St. Theresa and she wouldn't be either if she was married to Stan.

(then)

Slacking off, for chrissake! He says I'm using AA as an excuse to stay on the phone with my AA friends instead of cleaning the house. He means cleaning up after him and his pig friends. They come over to watch ESPN on Stan's big screen and drop food all over the floor and the house reeks of beer and I'm supposed to follow them around with the vacuum? Please. 'Sides, Evelyn gets nuts when I use the vacuum 'cause I roll up the cord different than she does, so then she yells at Stan and that's MY fault? Ha!

(then)

STAN'S the one who invited his mother in, God bless her, and now she gets on his nerves with her complaining so I've got to turn into Martha Stewart so that HIS mother will go home. I don't think so, dammit!

(then)

Oh, I forgot...I'm Rachel and I'm a grateful alcoholic.

Cassie

Thank you, Rachel. Feel better?

Rachel

(laughing)

Yeah, yeah, I do.

Cassie

Leslie.

Leslie

I had a wonderful week, Ladies, my best week sober so far. Last Sunday I went to a speaker meeting in Encino. The speaker himself was boring...he went on and on about sports bars where he did his drinking...all that faux macho-bull...a beer when the Lakers go ahead...a shot when they score a three...face down on the table by halftime...by the Final Four this guy had three DUIs and sixty days in County...I felt like I'd seen the whole season....

(pause)

But....

(pause)

I met another lawyer....

(quickly)

a woman. I might ask her to be my sponsor.
After the meeting we went out for coffee. She
told me that her firm has a once-a-week
lunchtime AA meeting. I couldn't believe it!
The firm she works for is really ginormous
and famous and they actually have a meeting
in-house! I'd rather die than let colleagues
know I'm an alcoholic. I've heard them
whisper about people they think drink too
much. I haven't heard a lot of compassion and
nothing at all about it being a disease. What
I've heard is disgust, usually from people who
pop pills every two minutes.

(then)

But Sarah, my maybe sponsor, says that her
colleagues knowing helps her stay sober.
Nobody ever asks her why she isn't drinking
and she doesn't have to make up stories about
taking allergy pills. She says she feels like she
has to work harder than anyone else but that's
more likely a woman thing than an alcoholic
thing and maybe not a bad thing. And she
says I should stop making fun of the Big Book.
I'm not making fun. I'm merely observing.

(one breath)

I went out with that colleague I talked about,
David.

(then)

We didn't actually go out. He called and came
over and we…well, you know.

(smiles)

I'm…he…he's surprising me. The first time I
thought he was just another litigator with his
pants on fire but he's not. He's smart and
funny and taller than I am and talks law all

the time which I do, too, so we're always interrupting each other and laughing. We're so much alike that....

(one breath)

David had to leave before eleven because he's married but I'm never getting married anyway so this could be the perfect relationship for me, don't you think? That's all.

Cassie

(quickly)

Coffee break.

Leslie, Rachel and Elena head for the coffee pot and the Oreos I'd piled on a plate. I sidle around the table, slipping into the chair beside Katherine's.

Cassie

How's the bones?

Katherine

Don't worry. I won't say a word to Leslie....

Cassie

I'm not worried.

Katherine

Then why is coffee break twelve minutes early?

Cassie

You caught me, Obi-Wan.

Katherine

I could tell Leslie she's heading for a big fat disaster that will wreck her life and ruin her sobriety but would she listen?

Cassie

I don't know.

Katherine

My granddaughter won't. She's going with a guy who treats her like dirt but she won't hear a word I say about him.

(sighs)

And she's such a nice kid.

Cassie

I'm so sorry.

Now I know why Katherine's so upset about Leslie. When we can't "fix" the dearest, we try to fix the nearest.

Cassie

Leslie reminds you of your granddaughter?

Katherine

Hell, no. My Becca's sweet as they come. That Leslie's a snob.

Cassie

Maybe she's a work in progress like we are.

Katherine

You can't make progress running in the wrong direction.

    (then)

Besides, Leslie's not strong like we are.

I laugh, indicating Katherine's walker and my latest fashion accessory, an attractive black Velcro back brace.

Cassie

Sure. In our spare time we wrestle bears.

Katherine shoots me a look.

Katherine

Nobody likes a smartass. You know what I mean.

    (then)

C'mon, Cassie. You can tell when somebody's not going to make it, can't you?

Cassie

I used to think I could. Then the people I
thought were going to make it went out on
benders and never came back. And the people
I thought would be gone after a couple of
meetings grabbed hold and hung on.

(shrugging)

I haven't a clue.

Katherine

The ones who are going to make it look you
straight in the eyes.

Cassie

So do the sociopaths.

(calling)

Coffee break's over.

The women return to the table. Leslie places a cup of coffee
in front of Katherine, piling up packets of sugar beside it....

Leslie

Here, Honey. Would you like cream?

Katherine

(surprised)

Gosh, thanks. No cream, just sugar is fine.
Thank you, Dear.

Leslie takes her seat. Katherine looks at me, her eyebrows raised so high they're hitting her caramel-streaked hairline. They're saying, who wouldda thunk it?

We're about to begin again when Terri, looking furious, whirls into the room in a flap of rainbow-colored scarves and a clearly bad attitude.

Terri

Okay, so I'm late! But it's not like I missed the big test or anything!

Cassie

Happy to see you, Terri. Sit down.

Terri sits down and promptly plops her head down on the table. Then she raises her head slightly, scowls and announces:

Terri

If anybody talks about God I'm going to leave. I can't take anymore of this crap about how God takes care of everything including coming up with the rent. He ain't done nothing for me!

Rachel

Who put a bug up your…in your ear? I hardly ever talk about God. I should but I don't.

Leslie

God knows I don't.

Elena

I pray a lot. At home.

Katherine

I'll talk about my Higher Power whenever and wherever I want.

Cassie

It's my turn.

(then)

I have no idea if God exists. None at all. I never have. I'm not being stubborn or willful or just plain stupid. I simply don't know.

(then)

During my first six years in AA I was afraid to say that. I was afraid I'd get drunk if I admitted that I didn't believe in God the way everyone else did. I was afraid that people at meetings would yell at me. Then one night a woman came in and started crying because she'd said she didn't believe in God and somebody told her she wouldn't stay sober if she didn't, so what could I do?

(then)

I said that I didn't believe in any God I'd ever heard about, so I'd made AA itself my Higher Power.

(then)

It's a pretty safe bet that I'll never be the last AA in the world still sober, so AA is a great Higher Power. A Higher Power is just something that's bigger than we are. We all have a

Higher Power that can kill us. One shot of scotch and my life disappears. So why not a Higher Power we can trust? For most, it's some version of God. For me it's The Group.

(then)

I knew a guy whose Higher Power was the tree in his front yard. When it got hit by lightening he picked another tree. Worked just fine. He's still sober.

Terri

(mumbles)

Weird.

Rachel

Aren't you afraid to not believe in God?

Cassie

Why would I be? If there's a God, he wishes me well or I wouldn't be sitting here sober. If there isn't a God, so what? I've got all of AA all over the world.

(to Terri)

There, Terri. We talked about God. Okay with you?

Terri raises her head. Tears smear her purple mascara.

Terri

No! I hate it here! You're all fuckin' creepy

with your fake smiles and "keep comin' back."
I hate it...I can't stand it but...I got nowhere
to go!

As one, everyone including Katherine, rises and moves to
Terri who's buried her head in her arms and is sobbing. Like
female elephants massaging the distressed one in their midst with
their trunks, we each pat the part of Terri we can reach. She
continues to sob and we continue to pat, making soothing noises.
We all know that some kind of healing is happening, even Terri
knows.

C H A P T E R   F O U R

MOST OF MY LIFE HAS HAPPENED BY ACCIDENT. I GOT married at eighteen which was a big surprise to me as I'd planned to go to John Carroll University and major in English. To pay for college, I'd gotten a job at the American Greeting Card Corporation writing greeting card verses. Writing appropriate sentiment that rhymes (at that time it all rhymed) and matches a pre-existing picture isn't easy. I'd stare at the watercolor of a perky yellow duck and finally come up with, "This little ducky comes to say, have the best, best, BEST birthday." On the scale of one to ten, this was minus fourteen. The only verse I ever wrote that I liked, was my all-purpose winter holiday offering, "Deck the halls with Matzo Balls." Oddly, it flopped.

Shortly after my eighteenth birthday, a man I worked with named George, asked me out on a date. I wasn't sure what to do because I'd never had an actual private conversation with George and didn't know much about him. From our group coffee break conversations, I knew he was from Boston (the accent would have told me that anyway) and Catholic, which was important because I wasn't allowed to date anyone who wasn't.

Our first date was dinner followed by a couple of confusing hours spent at the International Seven Day Bicycle Races watching a United Nations of cyclists go "round and round" an indoor track until I told George I was going to throw up. Inexplicably, he asked me out again. He was a nice man with a great sense of humor, so

I said yes to the second date but told him that he'd have to meet my parents first, the Rule of the House.

For some reason, this medieval custom didn't scare him off. He showed up the following Sunday at the appointed hour, was welcomed by my mother who showed him into our basement rec room where my father was watching the Cleveland Browns on television. There they remained, getting acquainted, while Mom and I stayed in the kitchen making pot roast and Dad's favorite, maple walnut layer cake.

By the time Sunday dinner was ready, my Dad and George, who'd clearly morphed instantly into my suitor, were football buddies. After George left, Mom went on and on about his good looks, good manners and "maturity," which made sense because he was closer to her age than he was to mine.

As we continued to date, George seemed to have only a surface grasp of my family dynamic which was a good thing because at its core, my family dynamic was dark and twisted. My father, beset with unpredictable rages he felt no need to control, was viewed in those days as "very strict." In those days, a kid could go to school with a black eye and bruised arms, and the nuns would look in the other direction, presumably upward toward God, who was comfortingly invisible.

Mom was a tiny Irish lady who cleaned house as though the Dirt Police could arrive any minute to throw her in jail if they found one speck of dust anywhere. If a new cleaner came on the market, Mom would march a mile in the snow to buy it. Our house reeked of Lysol. Outside of cleaning, Mom spent most of her time trying to devise stratagems to keep Dad calm. We were advised to greet him at the door when he came home from work, stay out of his way, distract him with questions about his day, *never* ask questions about his day, and on and on. All these schemes were futile so my sister, brother, and I developed our own: when we heard his car pull into the driveway, we'd run like hell, scattering into bedrooms, nooks, crannies, wherever. We'd hide, listen for his footsteps and imagine him mumbling, "Fe, Fi, Fo, Fum." Mealtimes consisted of casseroles, Dad yelling, and four tension headaches.

When Mom grew weary of her strategies, she'd try passing on the folk wisdom she'd learned from her very large family, none of whom we ever knew because Mom didn't drive and couldn't visit them and Dad thought his own family was visitors enough for us.

True, by the time we were old enough to wonder why Mom didn't have any relatives of her own, she'd been feuding with most of her family for so long, she could no longer remember why. Somebody had said something or done something or looked a certain way at her and, well, she wouldn't give the "bastid" satisfaction. We weren't sure what that meant, but occasionally wondered why the Irish side of the family seemed to be composed of all "bastids." In adult years, when we met some of these relatives, we found them to be (surprise) not only normal but charming, not "bastids" at all. When we pointed this out to Mom, she said, "Well, they changed. I been praying for them for years and they changed." We'd quickly agreed as we always did with Mom because it was simpler. If we didn't agree, she'd tell us she'd never speak to us again, then she'd instantly regret saying it. Then we'd all have to go through a long rigmarole while she devised an excuse that "forced" her to speak to us against her will, an exhausting process. So we'd agree to her face and laugh later, especially at the folk wisdom.

For instance, one warm summer evening, my sister and I, both adolescents, were sitting on the front steps when Mom burst through the screen door screaming, "Get up! Get up! You're both having your periods! When girls who have periods sit on cement, they get TB!" We got up, ran around to the back of the house where we fell into the petunias, laughing. Mom had a million of these bits of wisdom and believed every one. She loved St. Theresa the Little Flower and she loved George. "God only knows why a man that smart is interested in you."

But he was. And he even thought that I was smart, which made me feel competent for the first time in my life. I looked upon him as a person that any girl with half a brain would be lucky to love even though I'd had zero experience with love and the feelings associated with it. The closest I'd come had been dating the brother of a girlfriend who'd fled to the seminary after our seventh date. I didn't count an intense crush on the late, great James Dean, who was already both late and great before I developed the crush. Not exactly the basis for mature decision making, but great for accidental serendipity, my modus operandi.

One night my brother came home to find me sitting at the kitchen table smoking and staring into space. He pointed at the doors separating the kitchen from the living room. He told me he didn't know those doors could close. I told him that Mom had had some guy come in that afternoon to plane the doors so they would close.

His eyebrows flew up. "What's going on in there?"

We could hear the muffled voices but not what was being said.

I shrugged. "From what I've heard, George is in there asking Mom and Dad for my hand in marriage."

"Hand?"

"That's what Mom said. George called Dad at his office and made an appointment."

Jim sat down at the table across from me. "You're kidding me. Right?"

"Nope."

"You're too young to get married."

"I don't feel too young. I feel old," I sighed. "Don't you like George?"

"I like him a lot. He's a great guy but what's the rush?"

"Remember two months ago when I told Dad I wanted to move out and share an apartment with Nancy Horton from work? And he said that the only way I'd ever get out of this house is on the arm of my husband?"

"I remember."

"I have to get out of this house."

"What about George? What does he think?"

"Last night when we were talking, I was telling him that I want this and I want that, or maybe this...or that...maybe. He just laughed and said I'm too young to know what I want but while I'm finding out, he'll take care of me."

Jim grinned. "I'll bet he used to bring home battered kittens."

"Just like you do."

Just then my mother opened the newly planed doors. "Get in here, Joyce. You're engaged."

The night before my wedding, my mother came to my room, insisting that because she'd never told me about the birds and the bees, she had to do it right then or my wedding night would be too much of a shock. She thought I might have a heart attack and die like a cousin her mother had told her about who'd died of fright the first time she saw her husband naked. Embarrassed beyond words, I quickly told Mom that I'd read a book on the subject at the Parma Public Library which was true. I'd learned all I knew of sex education sitting on the floor of the stacks, hiding out from the librarian.

Relieved, Mom said, "Thank God," and hurried out of the room, the last of her motherly duties accomplished.

We had a big church wedding. Single women who worked with George cried at his topple from eligibility and hissed at me as I went up the aisle. I was oblivious to the soap opera swirling around us as was George, who'd been for years his office's object of female desire without ever knowing it. Since his mother had died young, and he had no sisters, feminine ways were and stayed a mystery to him. He took fluttering eyelashes and flirtatious glances as personal tics like rapid eye blinking, never knowing they were directed at him for a reason.

In the next four years, we had three children, two boys and a girl. This, of course, was a complete surprise to me since a doctor had told me when I was seventeen that my uterus was so severely tipped, I'd have a difficult time getting pregnant.

They were crammed so close together in age, that at one point, I was putting diapers on three children every night. Having kids close together is hard when they're babies and toddlers. But it gets easier as they get older. Eventually they're all teenagers at the same time and since I like teenagers, and mine were great teens, that part was fun. Now as adults, they are people I respect and admire as well as love. And most certainly, the children I didn't plan but who just "happened," are the best part of my life.

But back then, having three kids at the age of twenty-two was beginning to feel like a lifestyle that might be getting out of hand. Quick calculations on a torn grocery bag told me that if I continued to have children at this rate, by the time I hit menopause, I'd have thirty-seven children. Clearly, I'd run out of names to give them all and my poor tipped uterus would fall out onto the floor.

I told my mother that I was going to go on The Pill.

"Catholics can't use The Pill. You'll go to hell."

She advised me to use the birth control she'd used so effectively. "Stop sleeping with your husband," she said.

Aha, I thought, that explains a lot, but not why a twenty-two-year-old woman would give up sex after four years of marriage, which at the time was the dumbest thing I'd ever heard in a lifetime of hearing dumb things, most of them directed at women. Only later, years later, did I feel the compassion I should have felt then for the women who'd gone before me, the wives, mothers, nuns, and single women who'd been raised to believe that their warm hearts and singular passions were intrinsically debased and debasing.

It was years after that when I'd been sober for months that Mom confided, in one of her rare bursts of candor, how many of her relatives had died before age thirty of her family's deadliest health combo – alcoholism and TB. She'd name a name unknown to me: Aunt Elsie, Uncle Shaun, Aunt Peg, Brian the bartender cousin, and describe them with the same phrase, "They got TB and then the drink took 'em."

TB seemed to be a family weakness going way back to the nineteenth century mists and bogs of Ireland but the real epidemic of course was "the drink."

"The drink took 'em" is as good a description of alcoholism as I've ever heard. Of all the places drink took me, none were more appreciated than some of the AA groups I joined by accident.

I knew at my first meeting that AA was the key to my sobriety. ALL of AA, not just one particular group. However, I chose my Home Group carefully, wanting to belong to the same group as my sponsor and the people with whom I felt most comfortable. At first, I didn't feel comfortable because there was no one in the group even close to my age, mid-twenties, and there were very few women.

At my first few meetings I assumed that every woman there was an alcoholic but soon discovered that there were only four of us. The rest were the wives of the alcoholic men who accompanied their husbands to meetings. Men who accompanied alcoholic wives to meetings were scarcer than the proverbial hens' teeth. I met only one in my first year.

In the '60s and '70s, most women married to alcoholic men stayed with them, at least in the still traditional suburbs. Men married to alcoholic women more often abandoned them and with them, the kids. Few women found AA or any treatment at all for alcoholism. The stigma on women was far too great. Women were far too ashamed to ask for help. The people around them who knew what was wrong, their families, clergy, and doctors, avoided any mention of the "problem" for fear they would have to deal with it. Often men were advised to "try" AA. Very few understood AA at that time, viewing it as a place for those who were one step out of the gutter. Career women or suburban housewives were seldom referred to AA unless they had an enlightened doctor or friend.

An incident at my third meeting (just before I asked Alice to be my sponsor) illustrates the attitude at the time. The meeting had just ended. I was waiting to speak to Alice who was engaged in a lively conversation with her husband, John, and another AA couple when an attractive middle-aged woman sat down next to me.

"Hi," she said with a smile.

"Hi. I'm Joyce," I responded.

She leaned in closer. Her voice was low and almost soothing. "You know Dear, I can understand how a man can drink and lose control of his drinking. What I can't understand is how a woman could sink so low."

She got up and swished off, leaving me stunned. Suddenly my safe haven felt as unpredictably dangerous as my father's kitchen. I'd been sucker-punched and at an AA meeting!

I got up slowly and left without speaking to Alice. I got in my Woody and headed for the High Level Bridge, the steel ribbon connecting the East and West sides of Cleveland. I wanted to be back at the hospital, the only safe haven left.

As I approached the Bridge, I felt a burning pain in my chest. It took me a minute to know I was angry. Very angry. How dare that woman say that to me! Who the hell did she think she was anyway? Did she think she could run me off just like that with ugly mean words? Was I going to let her chase me away from the one thing I wanted more than anything else, sobriety? Hell no.

I turned the car around and went back to the meeting. Alice was still there, cleaning up. I told her about the woman and what she'd said. Alice scowled. "Where is this bitch?"

I didn't see her. "Gone home, I guess."

Alice said that at the next meeting I should point her out and Alice would have "a little chat" with her, then added, "There's a double standard, Kid. No use complaining about it. And God help you if you drink about it. Then it's your sobriety you've thrown away and for what? Just because ignorant people don't know what the hell they're talking about? You have to ignore them because they don't matter. They can't hurt you, they can't help you. They're useless to you." Then she laughed. "Half the women here think that we alcoholic women are after their alcoholic husbands. God in heaven, who'd want them?"

Alice never had her "little chat." I never saw the woman again. But I've always been thankful for her. With a few words, she'd turned a commitment I'd made tentatively into a commitment that was rock solid and permanent. I'd claimed my sobriety as "mine," only mine, not to be tampered with by any one person or circumstance.

So that was my home group by choice. Others I fell into.

At one time, I was working in an office on Vine Street in Los Angeles. It was the first job I'd had since an automobile accident had required several surgeries, a bone graft and a cast on my right leg that ran from my toes to my hip.

I couldn't drive for fifteen months which made me chronically grumpy. At that time my favorite line in the Big Book became "We are not saints." I discovered that I could simultaneously be sober and grumpy so long as I went to enough AA meetings. I knew I was pushing the envelope grumpiness-wise but cut myself slack because as an AA friend said, "You haven't even mentioned drinking."

Of course I hadn't. Every time I pictured myself drinking, then attempting to go anywhere on my crutches, I'd picture the inevitable, me clopping and weaving wildly down the street, then going ass over teakettle into the hedges. Didn't I have enough trouble with an aching leg and itchy cast?

On one of those days on Vine Street, I called the AA Central Office and asked for the location of a noon-time meeting close to work.

"How close?" asked the helpful volunteer.

"Very close," I said. "I'm on crutches."

"Hmmm. How far can you crutch?" she asked.

"About four blocks. Then I have to lie down and get my leg higher than my heart because my leg swells and the skin starts to burn."

"Really? Where do you lie down?"

"Wherever I am. Usually the sidewalk. I prop my leg against a building or bus bench."

"Don't people step on you?"

"I whistle. They go around."

"Is this true?"

"Every word."

"How long have you been sober?"

"Fourteen years."

"That's great! I've got eleven."

"Good for you!"

"Look, I don't usually say this but you've been sober a long time. Why don't you just wait and go to a meeting when a friend can drive you," she said kindly.

"Hmmm. Well, I'm beginning to think that my grumpiness is turning into a dry drunk," I answered, sharing a concern I'd had for days. A "dry drunk" is when a sober person begins to act with a certain amount of irrationality, with the next stop the liquor store.

"Aha," she said, and quickly found an address and wished me luck.

Ten minutes later, I was crutching up Vine Street toward a lovely old church of unknown denomination. A large sign on the front said, "Welcome All."

The meeting was in a large cool place called the Community Room. There was one very long table, and around it, women were listening to one of them share. The meeting had already started. They saw me and moved down the table so I could sit in the closest chair. I sat down and listened.

It didn't take me long to realize that most of the women in this particular group were prostitutes. I was hardly surprised.

Noon on Sunset and Vine? The location was right and the time of day was right. What was amazing to me was the determination of these women, some of them quite young, to find and maintain their sobriety in the most difficult of circumstances. Some, like women in AA groups everywhere on the planet, wanted to get sober for the sake of their kids. Others wanted to get sober in order to leave the life they were living. Like all of us, they were sick and tired of being sick and tired.

At their core, the issues they talked about were the same as I heard at every other women's group. Abusive relationships are abusive relationships whether the abusive partner is a husband, boyfriend, girlfriend or pimp. A broken heart hurts regardless of race, creed, color or profession. Illness and the inability to get well, has the same dire results whether it's caused by ignorance, neglect or poverty. Sick is sick. Broken relationships with families are mourned forever no matter how hard we try to leave them behind.

The women in this group shared about lives I could barely imagine and welcomed me and my sharing without hesitation. I never once felt "outside" in that group, never once felt that what I had to say wasn't heard even though my experience was as different to them as theirs was to me. We were all women alcoholics trying to stay sober and that's all that mattered to them and to me. I learned a lot from these ladies, primarily that people who were living lives that would destroy me could still want to get sober and did, every day, with each other's help and AA. They gave me new strength and an appreciation for the kind of tenacity that focuses on the goal and ignores the surroundings.

I went to that meeting every week until I finished that particular writing assignment. Along with me, there was another regular who wasn't a member of that particular community. She was a very famous movie star who came every week to share her ongoing battle with alcohol and clinical depression. Evidently the fog of her depression had led her to believe that prostitutes never go to the movies, therefore no one at the meeting would recognize her. Not being recognized was important to her even though her arrests for drunk and disorderly had been splashed all over the tabloids. Such are the delusions of alcohol and clinical depression. She needn't have worried. Not one of us at the meeting ever even hinted that we recognized her.

Acknowledging celebrities as celebrities at AA meetings is considered very bad form. Naming names is even worse, strictly forbidden. Anonymity is taken seriously.

I've always felt that though my own anonymity is mine to keep or not, keeping the anonymity of everyone else in AA is not optional. There are AA meetings, especially in certain cities, where many public figures attend. AA manners decree that celebrities and public figures be treated like every other alcoholic who's come to a meeting seeking sobriety. Those few who make the mistake of acting like either fans or constituents are usually very new and /or hopelessly immature. Very soon someone will take them aside for a "chat" and newly informed, the offender won't do it again.

The point of anonymity is obvious. Even in this "Enlightened (?) Age," there are still people who upon hearing, "I saw the Archbishop of Wahoo Alaska at my AA meeting," will go bananas, demanding that Wahoo find another top clergyman.

Of course, nowadays we have the phenomenon of celebrities' publicists announcing the celeb's entrance into rehab as though it was a stop at a spa before a world tour. I understand the need to control the news before the tabloids turn the story into "Celeb/Addict Devouring Small Children, photos page 22," but Jeez guys, give yourselves a break. Slip in the back door if you can. You need time and space to get sober, not flashbulbs going off in your face or the creepazoid press lurking in the bushes.

AA is the only place in the world where you can sit next to a person whose movie you saw last night, with politeness dictating that you show no sign of recognition. Along with the rest of its many virtues, AA is democracy in action.

For a time, my crutches, which I named Fred and Ethel, took me to a meeting dominated by a guru wannabe. She resembled the actress Nancy Marchand during her impeccably groomed

Lou Grant years, long before her disheveled decline into monster Mafia-momma in *The Sopranos*. Wannabe Guru sat at the head of the table, knitting like Madame Defarge and commenting on every share. Stern and opinionated, she thought of herself as keeper of the flame though whose flame she was keeping besides her own was anyone's guess. Her group seemed devoted to her but afraid of her as well, the perfect set-up for a Wannabe Guru. Anyone can stand up in the town square and shout their beliefs but a guru can't be a guru without followers.

It's easy to see how a Wannabe Guru can happen. Nobody comes to AA because their life is working out in perfect and wondrous ways. No one walking through the door for the first time ever announces how well he/she is doing and how their own brilliant ideas have made him/her a roaring success.

Rather, we fall through the door, the walking wounded with no idea of what to do next. We're hoping that someone will tell us. Better yet, will someone please show us? Even better, take us by the hand and gently guide us through every minute of every day? In other words, "Please Sir or Madam, I'm so severely f****d up, I want you to assume all responsibility for me, pick me up and carry me, tell me when to get up and when to go to bed and what to eat for lunch every day."

This is the first phase of sobriety when the only person we can't trust is ourselves. This is rehab, detox, the first thirty days, whatever you want to call it. As we go on and our sobriety and understanding deepen and we trust ourselves more, we're supposed to move on from this phase. The vast, vast majority of us do. Very occasionally, we find a group whose growth has been stunted by a Wannabe Guru, an ego-driven personality with a need to dominate. In a perfect world, a good therapist or tough sponsor would help them see that need for what it is, a part of their illness. In the real world, Wannabe Gurus don't go to therapists or seek out tough sponsors. It's more fun to stand in the spotlight giving orders and passing judgments.

Things came to a head in this group one evening when a woman shared the problems she was having with early menopause. She said that her doctor wanted her to start hormone replacement therapy. Wannabe Guru interrupted with, "You can't do that. Hormones are mood altering drugs."

What? In whose world?

Then it was my turn. "Hormones are not mood altering drugs," I said. "They make you feel better but that doesn't make them mood altering."

"Anything that makes you feel better is mood altering," Wannabe insisted. "We can't take any kind of drug at all. If we do, we're not sober."

Interesting. If you wait long enough, a Wannabe Guru will reveal his/her extreme side and actually Start Making Up Their Own Rules.

"What about aspirin?" I asked innocently.

"No aspirin!" she pronounced. "It's a drug."

Around the table, women stared at each other. Where was it written that we couldn't use aspirin? Had Wannabe ever had a fever? The light was beginning to dawn.

"And what about anesthesia?" I asked. "What about surgery? Is the doctor supposed to hit us over the head with a rock?"

"No anesthesia," Wannabe said firmly.

"For God's sake I had my appendix out!" one of the women said. "Was I supposed to bite on a bullet? You're nuts!"

Wannabe paled. She could feel her self-assumed power leaking from her. She opened her mouth, then shut it.

It was still my turn. "In my opinion and only in my opinion," I said, "none of us is going to get out of this life alive. Before we go, most of us will be sick and need medicine. Some of us need it now. Isn't one point of sobriety to grow up and learn to take the medicine we need as directed, just like everyone else?" I tapped my cast with Ethel. "In the hospital, they gave me morphine for forty-eight hours and I was glad to get it. Since then, it's been two Advil three times a day. Soon it'll be twice a day and then once and then nothing. Anyone who wants to tell me that the medicine I was given after the car crash somehow ended my sobriety and I have to start over, is going to get whacked with my crutch."

Nobody did. Weeks later at a speaker meeting, a man I hardly knew hinted that I might think about changing my sobriety date but fled when I bared my teeth and growled at him.

After a few more meetings Wannabe wandered off in search of an insecure group in need of a Guru. For all I know, she's still searching. If you see her, run. She's a poor soul with a screwy agenda, and she'll do you no good.

A wise person once said, "Home is the place where when you go there, they have to take you in."

One definition of "home" is AA. Walk through the door. We'll take you in. Makes no difference what neighborhood we're in, upscale, downscale or no scale at all, walk through the door wanting sobriety and you're in a roomful of people who want to help.

No exceptions.

During my early bewildered still-in-the-psych-ward-getting-lost days, I would study my gas station map, trying to find a nearby meeting that I could reach without turning too many corners. Never good at maps, I was further hampered by a new neurological quirk, the inability to distinguish right from left. Though this passed in time, at that moment, it made driving a serious problem. A helpful nurse suggested that I substitute north and south or east and west for left and right. I laughed merrily. Was the woman daft? If left and right was algebra, then north, south, east, and west was advanced calculus.

When the map finally revealed an East Side meeting that required only one turn at the corner of Prospect and Huron, I was very excited. I might actually get to a meeting on time. Dressed in my usual black slacks, black sweater and black coat, a style George had dubbed Mafia widow, I scraped the snow off my windshield, hopped into the Woody, and headed in the right direction.

At the corner of Prospect and Huron, I turned left when, of course, I should have turned right, then blithely drove along admiring the silhouettes of industrial buildings until the buildings became scarcer and farther apart. I was just beginning to worry when the street I was on suddenly dead-ended in a weedy parking lot on the edge of Lake Erie. Where the hell did that lake come from? Where was I, besides lost again?

I turned around and drove back the way I'd come, this time ignoring the buildings. When I came to the corner of Prospect and Huron I kept going. Finally I found the right place. The sign out front announced, "Garden Valley Community Center," a pretty name for a community center on the lower east side of Cleveland not far from the High Level Bridge but a world away from any garden I ever saw.

I parked, went in, found the right room, slipped in and found an empty chair between two women. This was a speaker meeting, both men and women. A man was speaking. He was talking about his overly inflated ego which, in his opinion, had been the source of all his problems since birth. To illustrate his point, he told of an incident from his childhood. He said that with several kids and two jobs, his mom was always overworked and his grandma continually frazzled. He said that he'd selfishly ignored their problems in a constant bid for attention. To that end, he'd hidden in a closet one day hoping that Mom or Grandma or both would come looking for him. After half a day had gone by, he'd crept out and gone to find Grandma in the kitchen bathing the baby. He'd asked her, "Didn't you miss me, Grandma?" She responded, "Ain't nobody ever going to miss you, Henry."

Henry went on to explain that even then, at the age of five, he was so egocentric, he thought that if he was missing, the whole world would stop to look for him. In my chair between the two women, I felt myself dissolving. I felt myself being five and so hungry for attention I'd be willing to spend half a day in a closet, so desperate to know that I meant something to someone, to feel loved by anyone, anywhere, I'd sit in the dark on a pile of galoshes, only to hear at the end of that trial that no one would ever, ever miss me. And then to reach the conclusion, once grown up and sober, that my normal human yearning for love was undeserved, a matter of "overinflated ego." I burst into tears.

The woman to my left put her arm around my shoulders. "You new, Honey?" I nodded yes, unable to speak. She patted my shoulder gently, then called out to Henry who'd stopped speaking and was just standing there, looking stricken. The woman said, "It's okay. She's new."

Henry's face relaxed. "Thank God," he said. "I thought maybe I said something."

After the meeting, the women to my left and right introduced themselves to me, curious about how I'd come to be at this particular meeting. I told them that I was a patient in the psych ward at the hospital nearby. I didn't tell them about getting lost and trying to turn only one corner. It was okay for them to know I was a psych patient, but I didn't want them to think I was nuts.

Those two women introduced me to three more "sober sisters." Before I finished my coffee, I'd been invited to the group's women's meeting on Wednesday evenings, same time, same place.

I looked forward to Wednesdays with those women. Though each group is different and has its own tone, I'd seldom found a meeting where the women were so remarkably insightful about life in general, their own lives, their addiction and recovery and, at the same time, so completely irreverent. Tears of empathy, shrieks of laughter, experience, strength and hope – all in abundance.

One night at the regular speakers meeting, the closed meeting room door opened and fifteen heavily armed Black Panthers filed in. They stood against the wall, arms folded over their bandolero looking very young and badass. It was 1968, and the Black Panthers were very much a part Cleveland's cultural landscape, applauded by some, vilified by others, viewed by most as just a more militant faction of the Civil Rights movement. This group of Panthers saw themselves as promoters of Black Pride and community protectors, and that's what they did as best they could without a viable plan. Most often the weapons they carried were empty for their own protection. The kids fighting in Vietnam had a better chance of seeing old age than an armed black kid in Cleveland in 1968. The moms I knew didn't want their sons in either Vietnam or the Panthers for the same reason. We don't raise our kids to go to their funerals even when we get a free flag for the coffin.

On this particular evening, the Panthers had grown tired of waiting for their meeting room to be empty. Evidently they'd decided that the wimpy AA people could be intimidated. So they stood and stared.

I could feel the tension building in the room. The AA people, once hot-headed drunks, now sober citizens on their best behavior, shot "don't mess with us" looks at the disrespectful young men. The young men glowered. The visiting speaker stared straight ahead and continued telling her story of growing up privileged in Kentucky horse country. Her storytelling became more difficult as the men in the group started to grumble. The grumbling rose. The Panthers stepped forward. I shrank in my seat, thinking that the last thing I expected at an AA meeting was an old-fashioned rumble, even in these turbulent times when peaceful events sometimes ended in a fog of tear gas.

Before this standoff could reach its illogical conclusion, it was ended by the woman who'd put her arm around me. She stood up and pointed at one of the Panthers, "Robert, this is an AA meeting. We'll be done at ten o'clock. Now you and your friends just go on outside and wait 'till we're done. You understand what I'm saying?"

For a moment, the Panther formerly known as Robert just glared. Finally he said, "Yes, Grandma." The Panthers filed out. We finished our meeting.

I became a full-fledged member of the Garden Valley Group, attending on a regular basis even after I left the hospital. Every Wednesday and Thursday night I made the trip over the High Level Bridge.

In 1968, many Cleveland/Akron groups still held to the tradition of Anniversary Dinners which meant throwing a group pot luck to celebrate the date when the group was founded. These pot lucks weren't AA meetings but an annual family occasion with the spouses, kids and grandparents of members as honored guests. We drank soda, water, lemonade and, as always, vats and vats of coffee. Long tables held casseroles, platters and Tupperware of every description, each full of delicious homemade food. I brought my best mac and cheese made with real heavy cream, cheddar from the Farmer's Market and way too much butter, the only way to make mac and cheese. I also brought George and the kids and introduced them to the friends they'd heard so much about.

It was one of those afternoons that later are remembered with a special fondness, smiles and sighs and "wasn't that nice?" We seemed to know it was special while it was happening because everyone lingered until the children, tired and overstuffed, got cranky. As I was rounding up my crew a newcomer with less than six months in the women's group, grabbed my arm. Her smile was huge. She said, sounding amazed, "This is what normal people do!"

Yes, sweetie, it is. And weren't we fools for ever thinking that "normal" sounded boring.

Several weeks later I was in my bedroom getting ready for my Garden Valley meeting when George burst into the room, looking distraught.

"Dr. King's been shot!" he said, then sat down on the bed and covered his face with his hands.

I froze. At moments like that, the first thought is always, "No, that can't be right." The universe that we live in tilts sideways. The ground under our feet shifts and our knees buckle. Our brains flail like a drowning swimmer. Rational thought is dry land, out there somewhere but beyond reach. Our mouths open but we can't take a deep breath. We are the wild-eyed girl on her knees beside the body of her dead friend at Kent State. We see but don't believe. The shock that protects us also short circuits our reason.

"Is he dead?" I finally managed to whisper.

"No," George shook his head. "But it's serious, very serious."

I sat down on my bed, still holding my shoe in my hand. No thought appeared. There was an ache in my heart just beginning but I pushed it away. Not yet. I can't handle this yet.

My mind skipped back three minutes to when everything was still normal. "I don't want to be late for my meeting."

"Are you sure you should go?" George asked very quietly. "No telling what might happen tonight."

"It's my favorite meeting. My friends are there," I said.

"You don't want them to think you were afraid to come," George said.

"Right." I kissed the top of his head. "See you later."

Only three months out of the hospital, my sense that I was surrounded by some sort of magical shield of protection had rubbed off on George.

Alcoholism is like the voyage on Noah's Ark. We alcoholics never travel alone. We drag everyone who cares about us with us whether they want to go or not. By the time we're either sober or dead, the loved ones who've stuck around, have done everything they could think of to help us. We've done nothing but resist them. So when we get sober, they're mystified. How did that happen? What was terribly wrong is now mysteriously right. Can I trust this "miracle"? Will it last? Why have we been so specially and specifically blessed? Not everyone feels this sense of protection, but we did and for a very long time.

"Be careful," George said.

I drove down Ridge Road, aiming for West 25th Street, and from there, a straight shot to the Bridge. My car radio was working even if my head still wasn't. There were bulletins and bulletins and more bulletins, all broadcast by shocked breathless people. Their voices skimmed along the top of my brain, their messages making little sense while I tried to think of what I'd say to my friends when I got there. Words came and went but none of them meant anything. There weren't any words. For the first time in my life I understood the human need to just "be there," to bear silent witness at an event that no words could describe.

As I crossed the Bridge between the two Clevelands, I felt a moment of both eerie calm and incipient panic.

I wouldn't feel anything like that again until much later, living in California, when the same disturbing sensation caused me to lift my head and sniff the air like a dog, just seconds before an earthquake.

Something was coming.

I crossed the Bridge, usually moderately trafficked but now deserted except for my Woody, turned right, then right again and pulled into the Garden Valley parking lot.

When I walked into the meeting room, a heartbeat of silence disrupted the buzz. I saw surprise play over faces already distorted by shock. My best friend from the women's group, "E.," took my hand. I hugged her. "I'm so sorry," I said. "This is terrible."

"It is." She led me to a side of the room where the members of the women's group who also attended Thursday Night were standing in a circle saying a prayer for Dr. King. One of them looked up and scowled at me. "We haven't got enough trouble. Now we've got you."

E. said softly, "That's enough. We're all feeling bad. And we're all scared."

The gears in my head very slowly resumed turning. What had I done?

In my desire to "be there" with and for my friends, I'd given them a big problem: a dippy white woman wandering through the wrong neighborhood on the wrong night.

They were called turbulent times for a reason. Not everyone believed in Dr. King's doctrine of passive resistance, his assertion that anger and violence brought nothing but destruction to all parties involved. We'd seen rallies turn on a dime into near-riots. My friends in Garden Valley had seen chaos up close and personal in their streets and front yards, unlike my neighborhood, where all white policemen patrolled all white neighborhoods and the turbulence was "theirs" not "ours."

Someone decided we should start the meeting. I slunk to my seat next to E. I crossed my legs, then twisted them in embarrassment. How could I have been so stupid? Didn't my friends have enough on their minds with their sadness and fear for Dr. King's life and their concerns for their own families without having to deal with me, their very own Pale Imitation?

A few minutes into the meeting, a man came in shouting, "Dr. King is dead!" Chairs toppled as members scrambled. I heard, "Oh no…oh God,"…and sobs.

The man at the podium whose name I can never remember shouted out that we should all stay calm and go home, right now. Get off the streets and stay off and nobody, nobody stop at a liquor store. That's the last thing Dr. King would want. Come back tomorrow and be safe.

E. took my arm firmly. "We're getting you out of here." Holding on to me, she waved at a couple of men who came over along with the ladies of the women's group.

The next thing I knew, I was being escorted out the door with a phalanx of people surrounding me. We headed for my car. I got in. E. leaned in my car window. "You wait until D. pulls his car up in front of you and I'll be in the car right behind you. We're driving you out."

I waited until D.'s car swung up in front and E.'s fell in behind, then followed D. out of the parking lot. My head had stopped working again. I absolutely could not believe that Dr. King was dead. I would not believe it. He couldn't be dead. We needed him.

At the exact center of the High Level Bridge, D. and E. honked their horns, made a U-turn and went back to the lower East Side.

When I got home, George was watching the television coverage. "He's dead," George said.

"I know."

I sat down beside him. We held hands and cried.

Chapter 5.

Welcome again. The meeting's already begun but I'm barely listening. My mind's somewhere else. This hasn't been a good day but I'm here, flopped in my chair like a wrung-out rag doll, my arms folded across my chest. The ladies come in, toss me a glance, read my body language and veer off, God bless 'em. They do what we wish our friends would do when we want to be with them but don't want to talk. We've all been there, haven't we? Needing a time-out because something has happened, wanting some comforting but pushing it away? Conflicted emotions, ye olde human curse. Were I the Creator, conflicted emotions would not exist and human beings would have durable, invulnerable stainless steel teeth. Ah, well.

Every time this happens, I feel like an AA newcomer, half-hearing, half-seeing, half-knowing where I am. So I go back to the first step. I am powerless over alcohol and my life is unmanageable. I can't tell you what a comfort that is. If life has thrown me a curve ball and I've lost my grip temporarily, I can sit quietly and listen until I feel grounded again.

We have a visitor tonight, a young woman I haven't seen before. Leslie greets her, something that normally I would do. When the woman came in, Leslie glanced at me, saw that I wasn't moving from my chair and immediately stepped in. What a pleasure it is to be dispensable. How awful it would be to be irreplaceable. Who can carry that burden?

Sometimes it's good to just sit and breathe and wait a bit.

And listen instead of talk. Rachel is speaking.

Rachel

I'm kinda used to not knowing what I'm doing except when it comes to the kids, but I always know what I'm feeling...no that's a damn lie...or maybe a mistake. I feel one thing then another and then, I don't know...I'm sure at the time, then it changes... (looks around) Can I pass the buck and come back?

Leslie

(smiles benevolently)

Sure. Katherine?

Katherine, who's sitting with her head on the table, resting heavily on her folded arms, raises her head slightly, just enough to glare at Terri, whose thumbs race madly over her phone.

Katherine

Girl, what are you doing?

Terri doesn't look up or stop texting. Katherine glowers.

Katherine

(continued)

I said, Girl....

Leslie

(interrupting)

Terri is texting. She's typing messages on her phone.

(to Terri)

Terri, it's rude to text at a meeting.

Terri looks up.

Terri

Who sez? That's not in the damn Big Book.

Leslie

Get real. They didn't have texting in 1935.
They barely had phones.

Rachel

Did you know that Bill Wilson called a party
line operator in Akron and asked for the name
of the town drunk? And she told him! I
wouldda sued.

Katherine

Then there'd be no AA.

> (to Terri)

Give me that phone.

Terri

You're not my mother.

I don't want to rouse myself but I do.

Cassie

Ladies, no cross talking.

(to Terri)

Terri, please put your phone in your purse.

We lock eyes. As I knew she would, Terri blinks first. As always, "please" is a magical word. Also, I'm bigger than she is.

Cassie

Katherine, do you feel up to sharing or are you too....

Katherine

(interrupting)

Cranky?

Cassie

I was going to say tired.

Katherine

I didn't hobble over here tonight to just sit like a stone, you better believe it.

(looking around)

Let me be plain. I've lost my fucking attitude of gratitude. That doesn't mean I won't get it back, but right this minute I don't give a damn.

(then)

The doctor I go to for arthritis...not that he's ever done anything about it, except tell me to take Tylenol and sell me this goddam walker,

now tells me I've got diabetes. Isn't that cute?
Just what I need. Well, you know what I
want?

(then)

You're expecting me to say that I'm asking for
the grace to accept the things I cannot change.
I don't want grace. What I want is a half
gallon screw top Chianti...no, I can't open a
screw top anymore...my fingers don't
bend...I want a box I can stab open on the
nail sticking out of my kitchen cabinet
door...because now along with a spine filled
with ground glass, I'm going to go blind and
have my leg amputated like Great Uncle
Antone....

Rachel

(interrupting)

Hey wait! Did your doctor say you're going to
go blind?

Katherine

He didn't have to. That's what happens!

Rachel

What *did* your doctor tell you?

Katherine

He gave me a pamphlet, *Living With Diabetes*.

Rachel

A pamphlet? That's it?

Katherine

He has a lot of patients, no time to talk.

Rachel

My mother-in-law has diabetes. She also has a doctor who talks. We'll take you.

Katherine

(looking bewildered)

Why are you cross-talking?

(to Cassie)

Rachel's cross-talking.

I glance at my watch. Much too early. So?

Cassie

Coffee break.

During coffee break, Terri pulls out her cell phone, heads for a corner away from the group and resumes texting.

Leslie and the new young woman drink coffee standing next to the pot. The young woman gestures a lot while Leslie listens solemnly, her head cocked to one side.

Rachel brings Katherine a cup of coffee and some cookies, sits down beside her and, I'm assuming is making arrangements to take her to the doctor. As Katherine eats the cookies, she seems to cheer up and become more amenable.

I wonder if she's eaten today. I've wondered before, but haven't asked. I don't want her to feel I'm checking up on her. But maybe ultimately it's better to check, even if she gets mad. Sometimes knowing Katherine is like sitting next to the ghost of my mother, comforting for two seconds followed by duck and cover when she's pissed off.

Cassie

Coffee break's over.

The women reassemble themselves around the table. As Leslie passes my chair, she leans over and whispers,

Leslie

Are you okay?

Cassie

Fine.

    (then)

Go ahead. You're doing a good job.

Leslie sits down next to the new woman. She eyes me quizzically, then looks suddenly disconcerted.

Leslie

What am I thinking? I've never run a meeting before...not this kind of meeting anyway....

    (to new woman)

Forgive me...I neglected to introduce you....

    (looking at a paper in front of her)

It's not in the format, but that's no excuse. We
always welcome newcomers. We are a very
small group.

Leslie pats the new woman on her shoulder so vigorously,
she winces.

Leslie

(continued)

Group, this is Kellie.

Everybody

Hello, Kellie.

Leslie

Kellie, you already know I'm Leslie and that's
Katherine....

Katherine

(interrupting)

She knows that. I shared.

Leslie

Right. And that's Rachel....

Kellie

Hi, Rachel.

Leslie

...and Terri and Cassie...and Christa's still traveling and Elena's baby has an ear infection, so they're not here.

Kellie

(smiling)

Hello, Seen and Unseen.

Leslie

(to Kellie)

Speak.

Kellie seems taken aback by Leslie's abruptness but only for a second.

Kellie

Thank you, Leslie.

(then)

I'm Kellie, grateful alcoholic. I'm twenty-three. Six months ago I had four years of sobriety.

Terri's head swivels toward Kellie. Four years of sobriety at twenty-three. Terri's done the math.

Kellie

I did everything wrong. At the time I didn't think so. I didn't think, period. First, I got a resentment at a woman in my group and it got bigger and bigger and I didn't talk to my sponsor, I just stopped going to the group.

(then)

This woman used to be on a TV show...you'd recognize her in a minute...she won an award...and she kept talking about what great times she had and the parties she went to and the guys she screwed...a lot of them were really famous and she said who they were...their real names, even the ones who were married. She made her life sound like the best episode of *Gossip Girl* you've ever seen only cooler because it was show biz.

(deep breath)

Then she'd turn around and tell me how lucky I was to get sober so young.

(pause, low voice)

I didn't feel lucky. I felt like I was stuck with a bunch of people like her who'd had a good time for years and years and then dragged their tired asses to AA when they were too pooped to party anymore. I started thinking about the friends I used to hang with and the fun we had. I forgot about all the bad stuff. After I hadn't been to a meeting for a while and being mad all the time, forgetting wasn't all that hard.

(lower voice)

I went back to the old places and guess what? I found my old boyfriend and he still thought I was hot! He even had his own business out in the desert, how 'bout that? He and his brother, who's even dumber than he is, were making meth. So Kenny is saying to me, "How 'bout it?" and I'm saying "Sure," like I've never been to one meeting in my whole damn life…

(pause, deep breath)

I'll tell you, ladies…you know all those things you're grateful you never did when you were out there drinking and using? Well, go back out there again and you'll do them, I promise. If you think you hit bottom before, that's nothing. There's a bottom lower than the worst bottom you ever heard of. There's a bottom where you don't feel human anymore. You're walking around dead but you can't fall over.

(sighs)

Then if you're lucky enough to end up in a hospital beat to a pulp and an orderly there is in AA, and he bothers to talk to you after you've cussed him out and if he calls some-body and a woman comes from AA, and with her help you drag your broken ass back to the Program, then ladies, you go to a meeting every goddamn night of your life. That's all.

The silence around the table is deep with echoes of Kellie's story. Finally, Leslie remembers she's "running the meeting."

Leslie

Thank you, Kellie. Rachel? You wanted us to come back to you?

Rachel

Uh…I was going to complain about Stan again but I think…maybe I'll just say how grateful I am to be sober and be here and leave it at that.

(quickly)

Except I'm going to need somebody to pick
Katherine up and bring her to my house so we
can take the bus to her doctor appointment.
My clunker finally bit the dust.

Cassie

I'll pick Katherine up and then you. We'll all
go together.

Katherine

(sighs deeply)

I'm such a burden.

Cassie

You sound like my mother.

Rachel

And my grandmother.

Leslie

And *my* grandmother.

Terri

(quietly)

I didn't have a mother.

All heads turn to Terri. Even Kellie who doesn't know her, senses that something is happening.

Leslie

(astutely)

Your turn, Terri.

Terri looks at her hands, folded in front of her. When she looks up briefly, she glances only at Kellie.

Terri

I'm a foster kid. I've lived a lot of different places. Some were okay. Some I don't talk about. Don't even ask.

(then)

I got tossed out of two for drinking. Don't ask how I got the booze. You need it. You get it.

(then)

In foster care, when you're eighteen, you get dumped. Happy birthday, get out. In some foster care families, the folks help you get ready but the folks I was with, they were too busy. So I just left.

(then)

I came here because my roommate made me promise I would. Her name was October. She worried about me. She got sick and they took her to a hospital. I don't know which one. They said she had leukemia. But she made me promise.

(then)

The folks had a VCR. We used to watch all the
Star Wars movies together. October used to
say that the force was with us. Yeah, sure.
What bullshit. But a promise is a promise.
When you only make one in your whole life,
you better keep it.

>   (pause, then remembers)

Uh…that's all.

Leslie

>   (warmly)

Thank you for sharing, Terri. We're so happy
you're keeping your promise.

Leslie looks around the table looking for the next person
who wants to share. I shake my head, almost imperceptibly.
Leslie's a lawyer. She can pick up a nuance, read a room.

Leslie

I'll go next.

>   (solemnly)

I feel almost guilty after what I've heard here
tonight but the point is that we share what we
were like, what happened and where we are
now.

>   (then)

I used to go home after work, most of the time
near midnight and drink until I passed out.
If I didn't drink, I was awake all night. On
weekends, I went into the office. Then I
realized I didn't have to get all dressed up to
go into an empty office on Saturdays and

Sundays. I could bring my work home. So I worked at home. Without even knowing it, I started drinking at home while I was working.

(pause, then)

That's not quite accurate. Of course I knew I was drinking, but I wasn't aware. Conceptually, knowing and awareness are worlds apart.

(then)

In any case, I made a couple of mistakes that cost the firm money. Not serious mistakes or serious money but enough to get the wrong kind of attention. One of the partners spoke to me. He was very low key but very direct. He said he didn't need to know the reason for my current slip in performance but he did need me to correct it immediately.

(then)

It wasn't difficult to connect my performance problems to my alcohol use.

(slowly)

I didn't want to see a mental health professional. It goes on your record. Even if you're seeing a shrink for something benign, like a fear of flying, it can be used against you. I've seen that happen.

(quickly)

Truthfully, I've done that myself. I mean used it. Against people. In court cases.

(then)

So I came to AA more for the Anonymous then the Alcoholic. I'm glad I did.

(smiles)

First, I give up alcohol without missing even
one day of work and then, I meet the most
wonderful man! I never even dreamed that
would ever happen! I'm happier than I've ever
been in my life!

    (then)

I haven't seen David for over a week because
he had to take his wife out-of-town to a
doctor. She has an auto-immune problem.
Lupus, I think. But he calls every day and
can't wait to come back. I can't wait to see
him. That's all.

Katherine

    (whispers to Rachel)

She was raised in Oz by Flying Monkeys!

Leslie

    (leaning forward to hear)

What?

Katherine

    (to Leslie)

Nothing, dear. I'm just complaining again. Oh
my spine, oh my elbow!

Leslie

    (sweetly)

Oh, you poor thing! Can I get you some
water?

Katherine

No thanks.

(holds up coffee cup)

I'll just finish my hemlock.

Leslie laughs along with the rest of us. Rachel tosses me a significant look. I nod. Yes, I know. Katherine definitely needs a doctor with more in his/her arsenal than pamphlets.

Leslie

Cassie?

Cassie

I don't want to share. I want to sit here and brood. But I'll share because other people shared with me when they were sad and angry. That's why I'm still here, warming this chair after forty-plus years.

(then)

I have a friend in Cleveland. Her name's Marjorie. She was one of the first people I met in AA. She brought the Big Book to the hospital I was in before I even went to my first meeting. For her first few years, Marjorie had a lot of slips. That's why she was delivering the book to the psych ward. Her sponsor thought it would be good for her to see "those less fortunate." Well, the psych ward scared the bejesus out of her. When the nurse rang the buzzer to let her in, she jumped six feet. Then she crept in, looking terrified as though she expected to be attacked any minute by a horde of raving lunatics wanting to eat her brain. Marjorie had seen too many zombie movies.

(then)

I'd been waiting for Marjorie at the nurses' station for over an hour trying to make small talk with E. Pomeroy, the nurse who passed out the meds. Since I'm bad at small talk and Pomeroy preferred patients stunned into silence on thorazine, this was not going well. I was very relieved to see Marjorie and, to be honest, really amused by her reaction to my home away from home.

Most people who visit a psych ward don't know what to expect. When I first got there, I didn't know what to expect. But the difference between me and the visitors is that they looked at the patients and saw a weird tribe, while I knew them by name and some of their stories. That made all the difference. To me, they were individual people who had real lives.

(pause, then)

I'm rambling.

(then)

Marjorie came in, threw the Big Book at me and ran for the door. Pomeroy buzzed her out and I didn't see her again for almost six months. Then Marjorie took hold of the Program, stayed sober and we became friends. Good friends.

(then)

Last Sunday, Marjorie's six-year-old grand-daughter Sammy was killed by a drunk driver in front of her house.

I close my mouth. I don't look at anyone. I know they look shocked. I know that the sharp intake of breath I hear is Rachel thinking of her children. There's more for me to say but I can't. Not this minute. All I can see in my head is the Christmas picture of Sammy that Marjorie sent to me, a grinning little girl in a snow-suit sitting on the steps of her grandma's house.

I've been trying not to think of Marjorie hearing the squeal of brakes and the sound of a crash, running out of her house to see Sammy bleeding under the car, and the asshole driver wandering around in the middle of the street, too drunk to know what he did. But I see that, too, because Marjorie described it just the way it happened, and I listened, as did all the AAs who rallied around her, hearts breaking for her.

Leslie

Cassie, do you want to add anything to that?

I shake my head "no."

Leslie

Well.

Leslie brings the meeting to a close. We stand, clasp hands, say the Serenity Prayer. This time Terri slips her hand into Rachel's.

Sometimes we want to go home and cry so that's what we do. Sadness can wash away in tears leaving a false sense of peace that's only empty exhaustion. The well fills again, tears drain it again, over and over until grieving is done.

Unfortunately, there are no tears magic enough to put out the anger that simmers and flairs just beneath sadness.

For that there are only two remedies. One is the ability to wreak terrible, swift and direct vengeance on the person or persons who caused this grief, i.e., murder in the first degree, always my heart's first choice. The other is a caring friend who knows we need to vent, even when we don't know it yet.

Rachel dragged me to Denny's for pie. Over plates of whipped cream and bananas, Rachel peppered me with questions.

Rachel

Is Marjorie staying sober?

Cassie

Yes, she is. She's yelling and screaming and carrying on, but she isn't drinking.

(then)

She told me she knows that Sammy can see her. She says she won't disappoint that child.

Rachel

Awww….

Cassie

I know.

(then)

Some airhead in her group told her she has to forgive the driver because he's a poor, sick alcoholic….

Rachel

(interrupting)

Fuck 'im!

Cassie

Exactly.

> (then)

Drunk driving's a crime. The laws should be tougher.

Rachel

I'd vote for that.

Cassie

This guy had two priors and still had his license. He said he needed his car to support his family.

Rachel

They all say that.

Rachel looks down, then away. I sense what's coming. I've heard it before. I've said it before.

Rachel

I drove under the influence a few times. Not a lot, but a few.

Cassie

Me, too. That was one of those lines I promised myself I would never cross, but I did.

> (then)

> Do you know how lucky we are that we didn't
> kill anybody?

Rachel shivers. For a moment, we're silent.

Lucky? Beyond lucky. Beyond blessed. Beyond any good fortune anyone can expect. Rachel couldn't have been more lucky if her dashboard Jesus had come to life to personally guide her through traffic.

And me? Whatever benevolence kept my neighbors and family safe from my insanity has my thanks forever. I didn't deserve that good fortune myself. I hadn't earned it. But the people around me deserved to be safe, and they were, no thanks to me. That's why when I'm occasionally asked to speak at a group, my topic is always Gratitude. I need to remember what I'm grateful for, what happened that helped me get sober, and what terrible consequences could have resulted from my drinking that didn't. I also notice that when the topic is Gratitude and everyone shares on that topic, we all go home feeling uplifted and mellow.

Maybe our brains have a Gratitude Groove. If we can just get into it for a few minutes a day, what a difference it makes! In my mind's eye, I see the Gratitude Groove as a fountain dispensing the mellowing, uplifting brain chemicals we all want so badly and never have found in a bottle or drug. And it's free, fellow depressives. Try it a couple of times. Turn on the Gratitude spigot. See how you feel. If you can't think of one thing in your life for which you feel gratitude, and some of us can't, either because of our whacked brain chemistry or because we have really crappy lives, make it up.

One day when I fell on my crutches and felt like I'd broken every bone in my body, the best I could do was be grateful that, so far that day, an asteroid hadn't crashed through my kitchen ceiling.

Am I grateful every day? Lord love a duck, no. There are days when I grouse and grump all day long, my ornery days when I'll be damned if I'll help myself feel better. But invariably after I've

wasted a day or so on that road, I straighten up and go for the
Gratitude. Why? It makes me feel good.

Rachel and I are both pushing mushy bananas around on
our plates, not really into the pie.

Rachel

So how are we supposed to feel about the
driver? If I was Marjorie, I'd never forgive him,
but...he's...you know...an alcoholic.

Cassie

Alcoholism is an illness. Drunk driving is a
crime. A drunk driver is a criminal. A criminal
belongs in jail.

(then)

It's as simple as that. Really Rachel, it is.

Rachel

But if he shows remorse...if he asks for treatment....

Cassie

(interrupting)

Marjorie doesn't want his remorse. She doesn't
want to forgive him...she doesn't care if he
gets treatment...she wants Sammy back.

Rachel

(sighing)

So would I.

Cassie

We have AA in jails. I went to Sybil Brand for
Women every Wednesday at noon for a year. I
empathize with those women. When the
experts talk about poverty causing crime, I
agree, particularly with women. I've heard
their stories. A lot of them never had a chance.

　　(then)

But, drunk driving is still a crime, no matter
what sad story the driver tells.

Rachel

　　(nodding, yes)

When I think of my kids....

Cassie

　　(leaning forward)

You know what makes me crazy?

Rachel

Life?

Cassie

Besides that.

　　(then)

It's the difference between the way people
look at smoking and drinking.

　　(then)

People have mounted crusades against

smoking and second-hand smoke. Tobacco people have been called to testify. They've paid huge fines. Laws have been changed. Children are protected from second-hand smoke. And that's all good.

(then)

But second-hand drinking, forget it. Second-hand drinking is drunk driving. And domestic violence. And child abuse. You'd think that the same insurance companies who lobbied for smoking legislation would be adding up the cost of second-hand drinking.

Rachel

Stan has a glass of wine every day for his heart. His doctor said he should.

Cassie

I'm not talking about people like Stan.

Rachel

Then who?

Cassie

Here's an example.

(then)

There's a bar on every corner. The purpose of a bar is to sell alcohol to people who want to drink in a social setting.

Rachel

(remembering)

Like being in a bar alone, sitting on a barstool, staring into a beer so the kids don't see me drinking at home. Some social!

Cassie

Well, you weren't alone.

(then)

But most people go to a bar to be social. Most of those people will never have a drinking problem. Their brains aren't made that way. But that doesn't mean they don't get buzzed.

Rachel

If only I could have stopped at buzzed.

Cassie

Me, too. Couldn't. Can't. Never will.

(then)

So, people have to drive to a bar to drink, then they have a few drinks and drive home again. This is supposed to be okay. BUT, drunk driving is a crime.

(sighs)

This doesn't make sense.

Rachel

And second-hand drinking....

Cassie

Less sense.

Rachel

Bring back Prohibition?

Cassie

Al Capone would rise from the dead to get his mitts on that one. Prohibition doesn't work.

Rachel

Then what?

Cassie

(shrugging)

I don't have the solution. Wish I did. But I think it might help if we start looking at second-hand drinking the way we do at smoking.

Rachel

And stop making those damn wine coolers and hard lemonade. They're like big soda pop traps for my kids. There should be a law!

Cassie

Maybe someday.

Rachel yawns big.

Cassie

Time to go.

(then)

Thanks for letting me vent. You've really
helped me a lot. I appreciate it, Rachel.

Rachel

Hey, no biggie.

We pay for the pie and walk out into the parking lot.
We hug.

Rachel

(continued)

Drive safe.

Cassie

You, too. See you Tuesday.

We get into our respective cars and drive away sober, no
menace to anyone tonight.

We drive with a heightened alertness knowing what can
happen.

C H A P T E R   S I X

For The Moms

WE ALL HAVE MOTHERS. WITHOUT MOTHERS THERE WOULD be no Eugene O'Neill plays, sitcoms or suicide notes. Without mothers, many of our lives would have neither a villain nor comic relief. Without mothers, countless numbers of us would never have met our personal heroes.

Mothers are the mighty shape-shifters, changing in our memories as we change, by turns giving, withholding, all-powerful and diminished. It's not our mothers who change, it's our perception of them.

Age changes our perceptions. When I was a kid and first saw Norman Rockwell's iconic "Thanksgiving" – benevolent, smiling, white-haired grandma serving the huge turkey to her gathered clan – how I wished that my two grandmas were like Rockwell's grandma, instead of what they were, dead and buried in Calvary Cemetery.

Lacking the cooking grandmas, I wished that my mother was the type to serve Thanksgiving dinner with a smile instead of her usual, "If I ever offer to do this again, just shoot me. Three days of cooking and no one else lifts a hand!"

I started cooking defensively at nine. Defensive cooking, like defensive driving, is about survival. My mother was Irish which means that all of our meals had just one recipe: throw everything in a pot and boil until gray, mushy and unidentifiable as food.

This is not an exaggeration. There are no Irish restaurants, no books on Irish "cuisine." This is a cooking "style" developed by people who, early in the twentieth century, died of starvation because the potato crop failed while all around them, the sea teemed with fish. The Irish are poets and dreamers and lovers and artists and fighters and talkers but they are not cooks. Luckily my dad was Bohemian. His dad came from Prague when it was still the capitol of the Kingdom of Bohemia and always insisted we were Bohemian not Czech. Czech or Bohemian, they know how to cook. I started early, learned easily and liked it.

The second I got married, I took over cooking for holidays and family occasions. For me back then, Rockwell's "Thanksgiving" was both ideal and goal. Setting the perfectly browned turkey on a table surrounded by family made me happier than winning any lottery could. I looked forward to a lifetime of perfect turkeys and homemade fruitcake, glazed Easter hams and rib roast at Christmas. I saw myself in the future, white-haired and smiling, presenting the thirty-pound bird to an ever-expanding clan. I blessed Norman Rockwell for his inspiration.

Now, many years later, I look at "Thanksgiving" with fresh albeit older eyes and I wonder, why in hell is that old lady carrying that immense heavy bird all by herself? What's up with those louts sitting around her table? Can't one of those men get up and give the old girl a hand? Has she spoiled them so badly that they think it's okay to be waited on by an eighty-something-year-old? Don't they know that her arthritis is killing her? Is that really a smile on her face or a grimace? Rockwell painted her from the waist up knowing that no one would want to see her ankles; ankles swollen so badly from hours on her feet in the kitchen that said ankles are hanging over the tops of her Keds. Fie on Rockwell for his perception that women are thrilled to serve 'till they drop. Fie, Fie and Fie!

Rockwell's painting didn't change but my perception did a one-eighty.

Similarly, my perception of my own motherhood changed with time, going beyond one-eighty and spinning in circles. At the beginning, with no innate talent for parenting, no acquired skills and a family model too dysfunctional to emulate, I leaped into motherhood with all the patience and sound judgment of your average ADD-afflicted teenager.

George was older but he'd had no sisters, so basic feminine functions were a mystery, if not a shock to him. To this day, he's grateful that our family was arriving at a time when dads weren't allowed in the delivery room. He looks at our sons and son-in-law with something like awe because they've marched bravely into the worst kind of combat, the battle over which you have no control. Not once has he asked the boys questions about their delivery room experiences. Ex-Marines tend to keep their combat experiences to themselves.

Also, George's mother had died at only thirty-one when he was eleven, and both of his parents were alcoholics, so he, too, was without a family model to emulate. Still, he *was* older, solid and steady, knew which end of the baby to feed and which end to diaper, told jokes to both ends and assured me every day that baby Paul would survive the Tender Loving Ineptitude of his teenage mommy no matter what my mother said. Without him, I would have shattered completely and my kids would have had nothing in their childhood resembling "normal."

For the first four years of motherhood, I was busy birthing, then for the next several years even busier sliding into alcoholism which, as we all know, is a full time job. I drank at home.

I know what you're thinking. How nice for the kids! They got to see their very own up close and personal Lifetime "social issue" movie of the week without ever turning on the TV set. They got to see it every day and every night for a very long time like a daymare/nightmare that just won't quit. They got to see and hear things that kids should never have to see or hear, all courtesy of the mom who really loves them and really damaged them.

When it comes to the kids, most alcoholic moms find the illness concept inadequate. We know that alcoholism itself is an illness but the *behavior* it causes is another matter. We know that we behaved badly. We know that we acted insanely. We know that this insanely bad behavior was often directed at our kids, the little people least equipped to cope with it. We know that it changed their lives and seldom for the better, though there are some people who become more resilient and stronger in the face of any adversity.

When we alcoholic moms in recovery think back to some of our behaviors, we cringe and our hearts hurt. There's no way around it. If we did insanely bad things, we should feel guilty. With kids, the insanely bad things needn't have been monumental. With kids, benign neglect can be as harmful as physical abuse. Saying "Go away, Mommy's tired," when mommy's really under the influence, can be as awful as not sending them to school or not taking them to the doctor when they're sick.

When I was first sober and still in the hospital, I asked a nurse what I could say to my kids to convince them that I wouldn't drink any more. She wisely replied, "Nothing."

She told me that by now my kids had heard all manner of rubbish coming out of my mouth including promises I didn't keep. She advised me to tell the kids, in plain simple terms that alcohol made me sick and I couldn't drink "grown-up drinks" anymore. She told me that they wouldn't believe me because they'd heard similar, though much more convoluted, statements before. I would have to *show* them by not drinking one day at a time, over days, weeks, months and years.

Of course I didn't want to wait that long. I wanted the kids to say, "Oh Mommy, how wonderful! All is forgiven!" I was new, therefore, knew little if anything.

I took her advice. Of course she was right. Their trust grew slowly. When I was having a soda, I'd see them eyeing my glass and wondering, so I'd invite them to take a sip. Invariably they did. Always they looked relieved, because, thanks to Mom, they knew very well the smell of a "grown-up drink." After a couple of months they stopped eyeing my soda. And I learned that when trust builds slowly, it sticks.

So what does the recovering alcoholic mom do with the guilt

from past bad behavior? Anything except drinking which will kill us and destroy our kids.

Therapy is good. Therapists knowledgeable in the alcoholic family dynamic can help the most painful heart heal.

AA meetings, particularly women's groups, are excellent. It's always good to discover that we're not alone in either our messy pasts or our guilt. We share and we listen and learn what others have done to cope. We remind each other that drinking will only make everything, including our closest relationships and our guilt, worse.

We recite the Serenity Prayer, which is, even without the spiritual element, a concise and complete Philosophy of Life. "God grant us the Serenity to accept the things we cannot change, the Courage to change the things we can and the Wisdom to know the difference."

What's past is past. It can't be changed. Not one day, one hour, one second. All the tears and the guilt in the world won't change it. It's over, done.

But the present and future, that's something else. In AA, we make our amends as best we can. When we've done something wrong, we say we're sorry. We do our best not to do it again. I've noticed that most alcoholic moms who've tried to make amends and become the mothers in the present they couldn't be in the past, have a pretty good relationship with their kids.

Some don't. Some kids can't forgive. Some moms can't either. Sometimes both mom and kids need (and deserve) more outside help and more time. Sometimes time just runs out, either physically or emotionally. What's happened has drained the kids to the point where they're too emotionally tired to try. They no longer want any part of us.

This is hard and it hurts, but we need to respect it. We gave birth to our kids but we don't own them. They have their own lives, their own opinions and their own feelings. If we think that they're wrong, even dead wrong, we may be right but so what? We've been wrong many times, too. We've all been stubborn, hard-headed and resentful. After all, we're just human beings, not saints. We're all subject to human frailty, the addicts and non-addicts. Human frailty is an attribute of human nature, not a fault. We can't *forgive* human frailty anymore than we can *forgive* the rainy day that wrecks our picnic. It's all part of the package. In a perfect world, we'd all give each other a break, especially the people closest to us.

Giving others the break we want for ourselves is a tough thing to do with consistency. I know, because even after forty-plus years, I still struggle with a less-than-perfect attitude about human frailty.

As for the leftover guilt (we in AA call it the "wreckage of our past"), what we share and learn from one another helps us stand our ground in the present instead of allowing our past to poison our future.

The mom/kid relationship is complex at best. Throw an addiction into the pot and you've got one stinky stew. If guilt about our kids helped get us into treatment of any kind, including AA, then we can be grateful for our capacity to feel guilt.

Guilt can motivate us to be better people. Without it, who would recycle? Or volunteer? Yes, I know that we're all as altruistic as Mother Teresa, but even she was avoiding the guilt of "not doing good" by "doing good" all the time. She was better at doing good than I'll ever dream of or try, but even she felt guilty because her faith wasn't "perfect" and because she couldn't minister to everyone. If even Mother Teresa felt guilty, I have to assume that guilt is part of being human, along with forgiveness.

A wise person once said, "Forgive everyone immediately, whatever your grievance, and that same forgiveness will come back to you."

Forgive everyone? Immediately? Why not ask me to climb Everest barefoot? What's that you say? It works? Call me back when I get my wings and halo. Okay, okay, I'll try.

Sometimes wise people are a pain in the ass.

In a perfect world, every recovering alcoholic/addict mom would have intensive therapy and so would her kids. Every person in an alcoholic/addict family would have an opportunity to rid himself/herself of the memories that haunt and the feelings that poison. In a not-so-perfect world, we each have to find our own way through that maze to find the help we need and deserve. But find it we must. All of us, parents and kids, deserve to feel better. We absolutely deserve to feel better. If we see a person having a heart attack, falling down in the street, we don't walk on by, ignoring him. We call 911.

We can't leave ourselves lying in an emotional gutter either. We can't ignore our own pain and its source. We need to call whatever 911 is available to us, parents and kids. For families there's Al-Anon, for kids there's Ala-Teen. For everyone, there's family counseling which is worth more than any video game, night out, or iPhone. Family counseling is the soundest investment we recovering parents can make in our kids' futures.

When talking about her own days of fractured motherhood, Alice would sigh and say, "Oh kid, if I'd known better, I would have done better."

We can all know better and do better.

I still roast a turkey once in a while. But now my daughter does most of the cooking. And the rest of my family helps to clean up.

Norman Rockwell painted his classic version of Thanksgiving dinner that kept me dreaming for years. But AA gave me the tools and the courage to create my own canvas of the ideal Thanksgiving dinner, with our ever-growing family sitting happily at the dining room table.

Chapter 7.

Welcome again to the Tuesday Night Women's Group.

Right now we're in Coffee Break which might be prolonged because Rachel brought homemade coffee cake. There's something about homemade bakery and real plates and forks and napkins that turns our usual stretch-your-legs coffee drinking into sitting around the table together. This usually happens only in small groups where everyone knows each other well (at times, some would complain, *too* well). The people who find small groups too intimate, have many other groups they can choose, from medium to large to "is this an AA meeting or is Bloomingdale's having a sale?"

To add to the genial atmosphere, tonight's topic is Gratitude. Those of us, including myself, who came here to Bitch and Moan, have instead been counting our blessings, even if we have to reach deep to find them. It sometimes comes as a shock to discover that we each have blessings to count, but a smile soon follows the shock and just like that, we're in the Gratitude Zone. It's a great place to visit and would be a better place to live but most of us, including me, hop the next train back to Bitch and Moan on a moment's notice. Human nature craves variety.

Elena's here tonight with baby Lucy. She's happy because Lucy wasn't really sick, only teething. Elena's been prying Lucy's little mouth open so we can all admire the tiny tooth just cresting above her pink gums.

I ooh and coo along with everyone else but, to be honest,

Elena's little Lucy turns my mind to Marjorie and her loss. I talked to Marjorie this morning and she sounds exhausted. She told me that grief-stricken is such an apt expression because grief knocks us down and then grinds us into the dust. She says that time, God's help, and AA will see her through. She says that right now, she's in a dark tunnel but there's light out there somewhere and she'll find it. Then she cried for a long time and said she felt better. She thanked me for calling. I don't know how she copes. Or how she can even talk about it. Grief leaves me speechless.

When people tell me that their Higher Power and/or God is helping them through a tough time, I'm always happy. Whatever the faith or belief, if it's working for them, then it's a good thing. If their faith helps them stay sober in this unpredictable, sometimes heartbreaking world, then it's not only good, it's a bona fide miracle. Marjorie's faith is her rock and her staff. It's her strength and her comfort. I bow with respect to its power.

I smile as I watch Terri trying to teach Katherine how to text on her phone. So sweet of Terri, and Katherine's responding to her friendly gesture.

Rachel and I took Katherine to see Rachel's mother-in-law's doctor. He did a slew of blood tests, found that her thyroid was low, stabilized her diabetes and suggested a water exercise class at the Y for her arthritis. Katherine is now describing herself as new and improved. She's certainly more chipper and most of her chronic crankiness is gone. Now she's busy telling other AA seniors that before they consider themselves as hopelessly afflicted with too many character defects to overcome, they should first have a physical. Those "character defects" may be sluggish thyroid or whacked-out blood sugar. Katherine, who can now get up and down the steps on a bus, is on a mission.

Terri is holding Katherine's phone under her nose.

Terri

See? You use your thumbs to type the letters.

Katherine

My forefinger works better. Can I just poke it?

Terri

(considers, then)

Yeah, why not?

Katherine

What do I say?

Terri

Whatever you want.

(then)

You can tell your friends what you're doing.

Katherine

All my friends are in AA. I see them all the time.

Terri

But not 24/7. You can text them what you're doing when you're not at a meeting.

Katherine

(thinks, then)

Like I ordered a shower stool from Sears and now I can take ten-minute showers?

Terri

(enthusiastically)

That's cool!

Katherine

(disbelieving)

Sending my grocery list would be more exciting. Who wants to hear about an old lady's shower stool?

Terri

(certain)

Other old ladies.

(then)

What if you haven't taken a shower for months because you can't stand up in the shower? And you've never heard of a shower stool? And don't know that you can have one delivered? Think how thrilled you would be to get that message.

Katherine looks at Terri, then nods.

Katherine

You know a lot for a kid, you know that?

(then)

Tell me, how do the people I send the message to, know that I'm me?

Terri

You'll probably send them to people who
know you.

Katherine

And if I sent them to strangers…?

Terri

They wouldn't know who you are. People talk
to strangers in chat rooms on their computers.
Some people make up their whole life story,
who they are, what they are…you have to be
careful.

    (then)

Why do you want to know?

Katherine

Oh, just something I saw on a Law and Order
rerun. I'm thinking that maybe I could volunteer to help the police trap pedophiles. I could
be a fourteen-year-old blonde.

    (then, shyly to Terri)

You probably think I'm crazy.

Terri

    (surprised)

I didn't know that people your age still want
to do stuff. Except watch TV.

    (then)

I think you should call the police and ask them.

>(off Katherine's dubious look, grins)

Really. You should do it.

Katherine

You think they'll laugh at me and that would be funny.

Terri

I don't think that laughing at anybody is funny. Foster kids get teased a lot.

Katherine

>(nods, then)

Where do you live, Terri? Somewhere decent, I hope.

Terri

>(laughs)

Do you mean decent like nice, or decent like do I live with junkies?

Katherine

I mean decent as in do you have a bathroom and do you have rats?

Terri

Yes and no. I have a bathroom but the rats

who live in the ivy aren't allowed inside the
house.

   (then)

I share a guesthouse on Fremont with another
foster kid.

Katherine

She's clean and sober?

Terri

He never drank or did drugs, ever.

Katherine

He?

Terri

   (gently warning)

Katherine....

Katherine

I know. I know. It's the 21st century.

   (grins)

Just so you know, honey, nothing's changed.
Boys and girls have lived together since the
Garden of Eden.

   (then)

Back in the day, the late Fifties, I lived with
Bobbie Montoya in his bedroom at his
mother's house. She thought I was a good

influence on him. *My* mom thought I was a slut. We had a real life West Side Story going on but without all that damn singing and dancing, thank God.

    (sighs)

After a year or so, Bobby dumped me for Nina Torres. Now that girl was a *bad* influence on him. But Bobby was nineteen. He wasn't looking for good influences. He was looking for a girl to knock his socks off. Nina was one hot socks-knocker-offer.

Terri

What happened to him?

Katherine

Don't know. I could have found out lots of times but I didn't. I felt like a fool. I had to go home and live with my mom and listen to her nasty remarks until I got married.

Terri

Would you do it again?

Katherine

If I was eighteen?

    (then)

In a minute.

Across the table from Terri and Katherine, Leslie and Rachel are eating and talking.

Leslie

(re coffee cake)

Delish.

Rachel

Thanks. Want the recipe?

Leslie

I don't cook.

Rachel

Not at all?

Leslie

I do take-out, delivery and boxes of frozen ready-made that I defrost. Mostly Lean Cuisine.

Rachel

(eyeing her)

You don't need Lean Cuisine.

Leslie

I eat two of them. And Ben and Jerry's.

Rachel
> (curious)

What about when the boyfriend comes over?

Leslie
> (smiles)

He doesn't come over to eat dinner.

Rachel

But sooner or later you'll be cooking for him.

Leslie

Why would I do that?

Rachel

Because we do that. Women do that. We feed
people.
> (then)

Sooner or later you'll fix him a snack and he'll
tell you how good it is even though at his
house at that very moment, his wife's cooking
a dinner he'll be too full to eat because of your
snack.

Leslie
> (scowling)

And you know this because…?

Rachel

Not from personal experience, Leslie, that's for sure. I got enough problems. You think you're the only person in a women's group that ever had an affair with a married man?

Leslie

Statistically, no.

Rachel

Well *statistically,* it all turns to crap.

Leslie

  (coolly)

Only if the woman wants to get married, Rachel. And according to you, marriage is all arguing and ESPN and doing what Stan wants to do. See? I listen.

  (then)

My apartment is immaculate. I listen to Mozart. I watch CNN. I eat when I want to and don't when I don't want to. I come and go as I please. I don't have to tell anyone where or when I'll be back. To me that feels like asking permission. I don't like asking permission. I'm madly in love with David but why would I want my life to change?

By now we're all eavesdropping on Leslie and Rachel. Katherine leans forward.

Katherine

Why would you want your life to change?

(then)

Hormones, Lady.

Leslie

Forgive me Katherine, but that kind of thinking is very outdated.

Katherine

You'd like to think so, but it's true.

(then)

From puberty to menopause, hormones run our lives. Same thing with men. We like to think we're making our own decisions, but it's hormones running the show.

(exaggerated sigh)

I love him. I miss him. I want him. I got him! I wanna get married. Oops. He's gone. I'm depressed. I can't live without him. I want to die. That son of a bitch took my hormones away! I'll have a drink. That'll show 'im. I'll have a couple. I can stop anytime. I'm drunk. I can't stop. Where did I go? I need another drink. Maybe I'll just sit here and die.

(shakes her head)

Now who's the asshole? Not him. Hormones, all hormones.

Leslie

Katherine, that's very…entertaining, but I'm a lawyer. I run on logic.

Elena

You're seeing a married man! What kind of logic is that?

Leslie

(patiently)

I don't want to get married.

Katherine

You will. It's hormones.

(then)

We don't know how crazy hormones make us until they all go away.

(sighs)

Or how restful life is without them.

(knowing)

Or how logical we become when they're gone.

Rachel

I'm going to hang onto mine as long as I can. My mom's skin got dry and thin as tissue after her menopause.

Katherine

Skin isn't the point! There are creams for your skin! I have a tub of Vaseline Intensive Care, for pity's sake. Head to toe every morning. Sinks right in. Skin's not the point.

My turn.

Cassie

Judgment's the point. That's what Katherine is saying. She believes that our hormones affect our judgment.

Katherine

Thank you. They do.

Cassie

I believe that. How could they not?

(to Leslie)

I don't believe in telling people how to live their lives. I'm no expert in anything.

(then)

Even if I wanted to, I wouldn't, because my sponsor Alice taught me Alice's Rules and they worked for me....

(then)

When I first met Alice, she told me flat out that if I was having trouble with my marriage, I should see a marriage counselor. If I was having trouble with my kids I should see a child psychologist. And so on and so on. Whatever the problem, I should ask the right expert and that wasn't her.

She said that all she knew anything about was staying sober one day at a time for thirteen years. If I had a question about AA or sobriety, I could ask her but ONLY if I came to one of the three meetings she went to every week. Then she'd give me fifteen minutes to talk after the meeting.

Also, I wasn't to call her after nine in the evening because she got up for work at five every morning. If I felt like I was going to take a drink, I could call her *anytime* and by God, I'd better. If I'd already taken the drink, I was to tear up her phone number and find another sponsor IF I ever got back to AA. She'd had enough "babies" break her heart, thank you.

(then)

I learned from Alice's rules and her attitude that if I stayed sober for long enough, I'd be able to set up some boundaries for myself. I'd learn that I deserved to take better care of myself. That I'd learn how to do that from AA and the experts. Judgment takes time, Leslie. Sober time.

Leslie

(impatient)

And you're telling me this because….

Cassie

You've been sober less than a year. That's not a lot of time.

(then)

AA recommends that we avoid making major

decisions for the first year unless we absolutely must. AA also recommends that we don't start a new relationship for a year.

Elena

Jump in before your head is clear and you're asking for trouble. You'll find a guy who's as screwy as you. The rocks in your head will fit the holes in his.

Leslie

That's fine for most people, but....

>   (hangs there)

Cassie

I know. You're a lawyer.

>   (then quickly)

Sorry.

>   (then, carefully)

Sometimes when we make major changes, especially the first year, some of us find it helpful to talk to a therapist.

>   (quickly)

Just as a sounding board.

Leslie stares at me. I can see her eyes hardening.

Leslie

I'm a sounding board for my clients. They pay

me a lot of money for my judgment. I'm doing
fine.

Out of the corner of my eye, I see Terri texting in a drum-
beat of thumbs. It's time to get back to the meeting.

Cassie

Coffee break's over.

Terri looks up from her phone.

Terri

I got a friend who wants to come next week.
Okay?

Cassie

If your friend is female and has a desire for
sobriety, bring her along. You don't have to
ask permission.

Terri

(excited)

Great! Next week she's here in LA with the
circus!

As we all look interested, we....

C H A P T E R   E I G H T

HOW OFTEN DO WE MEET PEOPLE WHO CHANGE OUR LIVES? Because I'm lucky, the answer for me is "all the time." In fiction, when incredible coincidence also takes a turn for the comic, most people say "enough already, I don't believe a word of this!" Only real life can make the people involved gasp and giggle at the same time.

For example, years ago I was a passenger in an automobile accident. The accident came about because my husband George Burditt, aka "George the First," had taken me to dinner to meet his Chicago cousin, George Burditt, aka "George the Second" and the cousin's son, George Burditt, aka "George the Third." During the course of my dinner with the three Georges, I discovered that Chicago George the Second and I had the same birthday. George the Second, an expansive politician, insisted that his son, George the Third, take me to lunch on "our" birthday since he wouldn't be in LA for that happy event. The third time he insisted, I felt I had to agree even though I didn't know George the Second or Third, and had planned a birthday lunch with two girlfriends.

I rescheduled the girlfriend lunch. On the designated day, George the Third and I drove off to find cheeseburgers and cake.

Going off an off-ramp, George the Third had a seizure. We hit the cement post that held the "stop" sign. The car rolled over on the side on its two left wheels, made a half circle, still on two wheels and crossed over the freeway, finally landing in a gully that divided the sides of the freeway.

Today that gully is a cement wall. Back then, if it hadn't been a deep gully full of tall weeds, I would be writing this through one of those people who channel the random thoughts of the dead from the great beyond. As it was, the weeds dragged the car to a halt.

George the Third went straight from his seizure into shock. Since he'd been rigidly attached to the wheel, his only injury was a cut on his forehead where it hit the rearview mirror. As George the Third stared straight ahead, I saw smoke rising from under the car's hood.

I knew that my leg had been injured because the pain was incredibly searing and terrifyingly horrible and my right foot was turned backwards. I couldn't move. I couldn't rouse George the Third from his shock. I was resigned to the fact that I was going to burn to death in this car with a backwards foot and bad attitude, cussing out George the Second.

Suddenly from out of nowhere, a young man carrying a fire extinguisher ran to the driver's side of the car, reached into the open window and popped the hood. He sprayed the engine fire with the extinguisher, then threw it on the ground. Faster than I could think about it, he'd opened the driver door and pulled George the Third out into the weeds where he lay on his back looking dazed. Then the young man came around to my side of the car, and opened the door with some difficulty because my door was wedged against the slope. He looked me up and down, then saw my leg and funky foot and told me not to move. He knelt beside me and smiled. "Don't worry, you'll be okay. I have a radio in my car. I called the police. They're sending an ambulance." He reached for my belt. "I'm not getting fresh. I was a medic in Vietnam. I'm just loosening your belt. Try to take deep breaths. You're hyperventilating."

He loosened my belt and untied my shoe but didn't try to remove it. Just then I heard sirens. I turned my head to look for the ambulance. When I turned back, the young man was gone.

A moment later, two paramedics were checking my vitals. I asked where the young man was. I wanted to thank him. The paramedics thought I meant George the Third. They hadn't seen another young man.

Later, George the Third told me that he had never seen a young man. So far as he knew, he'd dragged himself out of the car. And the fire extinguisher? What fire extinguisher?

Later in the hospital, I signed a form permitting the surgeon to amputate my leg. Just to be a good sport, I signed another form donating the leg to the medical school at UC. When they wheeled me into the operating room, I saw the surgical instrument table upon which there were a dozen saws, from teeny tiny floss-your-teeth mini-saw, to your basic Ace Hardware saw – down to a mighty-oak special. The last thing I remember thinking was that the young man had told me I'd be okay.

I came out of surgery with two legs. The right leg was patched and took over a year to heal, but it was there.

Over the next few weeks I thought about the young man. Objectively speaking, he was too young to have served in Vietnam, looking more like a long-haired surfer dude kid than a vet of that war. At that time, few people had phones in their cars and then only executive types who felt it their duty to be connected at all times to their offices. The fire extinguisher he carried was full size, not a compact just-for-the-car model. Who carried an extinguisher in their car back then anyway? And where was the car? Neither I nor anyone I asked ever saw it.

Who was he? I don't know. I didn't see any wings but I'm sure they were there, curled up under his flapping white shirt.

This is truth, and most definitely stranger than fiction.

Another example, this one more down to earth:

One day George came home from work and told me he'd met another writer, John Carsey, a terrific guy who'd just moved from New York to LA with his much younger wife, Marcy. They were staying in the same motel that George stayed in when he'd come to LA without the kids and me, to find a career in television. George suggested that I go over to Motel Crappy and meet Marcy. It's always good to have a new friend.

Knowing what a difficult time I'd had when suddenly displaced from my hometown to LA, I was eager to meet someone going through the same experience. Everyone I'd met in LA, from my brand new AA group to the PTA seemed to have been hatched from LA pods. They spoke of "back east" as if it was a galaxy far, far away. No one I currently knew in LA had worn galoshes for four months of every year or ever seen a firefly in their backyard.

I took my daughter with me. She was a bright and thoughtful kid with a penchant for startling observations like, "The reason we have skin is so our blood won't leak out" and even more startling questions like, "Where was I before I was born?" I spent years thinking about that one. I still think about it, in all of its terrifying implications.

When I knocked on the door of the motel room, it immediately flew open and Marcy appeared, flashing the most infectious smile I'd ever seen in my life. Her smile lit up her face and mine along with it. "Hi, I'm Marcy. You're Joyce. And who's this?" I glanced at my daughter. She was beaming up at Marcy.

When Marcy smiles, people smile back. Always. It's like a law of physics. It's the Force. Hers is simply the best, most spontaneous, cheering up, welcoming smile in the world. It should win a Nobel Prize. When that smile comes your way, you know that you're sharing your space with a good person and so she is, a very good person.

After a few minutes of chit chat I was, as always, at a loss for words. So I asked Marcy if she'd like to go to a nearby department store and…um…browse? I figured that most women like to looky-loo shop and at least she'd know where the nearest mall was located.

She said that was an…um…interesting idea.

We piled into my car and went to what was then Bullocks Department store. We had been in the store for five minutes and were wandering aimlessly through the makeup section when Marcy stopped and asked, "Do you really like department stores?"

I shook my head, "God no. I get in and out as fast as I can. If I can't find what I want in two minutes, I'm gone."

My daughter added, "She doesn't try anything on, either."

Marcy asked, "Why are we here?"

I didn't want to tell her that my social skills in the area of small talk were so minimal that my usual method of dealing with a new acquaintance was to keep us both moving. "Let's go for a hike. Do you ice skate?"

New acquaintances seldom became old acquaintances because, to be honest, they thought I was peculiar and unless they were athletic, too much work. Usually getting acquainted with someone doesn't involve either sweating or sliding across ice on your ass.

Marcy seemed to know I was shy.

We went to a coffee shop where Marcy asked me a million questions about life in LA. I answered as best I could since I was still learning the ropes myself. I told her my method of learning how to navigate the maze of freeways. Every morning after I dropped the kids off at school, I got on a freeway and just drove, trying to remember the connections from one freeway to the next. I learned the freeway system by the Hansel and Gretel method, first getting lost and then finding my way home. Marcy seemed to think this method was as good as any. She never once mentioned the word "map."

We became friends. The night of the day of the Quake of '71, Marcy and John came over to our place. There was no electricity yet so George and John grilled hamburgers outside on our tiny patio. Every time an aftershock hit, we all dived under the dining room table. The hamburgers were delicious even though we had nothing to put on them. The ketchup, mustard and pickles had all fallen out of the cupboard and smashed in a gooey earthquake mess on the floor.

At that time, Marcy planned to get her real estate license and I was about to embark on a career as a teaching assistant in a Special Ed class in Burbank.

This was a job I'd gotten by accident. A PTA friend and I were going out to buy cake mix to make cupcakes for school. She asked if I would mind waiting for her at the School Board while she took a test for a job as a teaching assistant. I said, "Test? I love tests. I'll take it for fun." The truth was I hated waiting more than I loved tests but nothing passes the time like a good test, so I took it. Later in the supermarket, my friend realized that if she got the job, she'd be working in a room with twelve kids all day long, and even worse, missing her soaps. Since the favorite part of her day was the moment when her kids jumped out of her car and ran into school, she felt that maybe she hadn't thought through her choice of potential careers quite well enough. "What will I say when the Board calls me?" she worried.

Lucky for her, I got the job. She later made lots of money selling real estate, scheduling her appointments around her soaps in an impressive blending of vocation and hobby.

My two years as a teaching assistant were the hardest, most involving job of my life. Too involving. As I got to know and love the kids, I wanted to take them all home. Their problems in school and at home pushed my "fixit" nature to the limit. I couldn't "fix" anything, not their various educational disabilities and definitely not their home situations, some of which were heartbreakingly traumatic.

I got an ulcer. I perceived getting an ulcer as what we call in AA, a "character defect." I felt that if I was working my program correctly, accepting the things I couldn't change, I wouldn't have a hole in my stomach. At meetings, I talked out my feelings. I also saw a therapist. Both helped. I also, reluctantly, left the job. Sometimes, retreat *is* the better part of valor.

I was at home one day, moping, missing my Special Ed kids and eating white rice, when Marcy called. I knew she'd gotten a job at a production company doing development, whatever that was, and liked it a lot. She asked me if I'd like to do some freelance script reading work. I said that I would though I didn't have the remotest idea of what script reading entailed. But I knew I had to do something and a job with "reading" in the title sounded too good to be true.

I went into the production company office where Marcy explained the job: she said that I would come in once a week, pick up material that had been submitted to the company, read it, write a one-page synopsis and then write a one-page recommendation or rejection based on a list of criteria she'd give me. "Goody," I said. "When do I start?"

Marcy handed me a pile of paper, ten submissions, everything from a two-page treatment proposal for a movie of the week to a six-hundred-page unpublished book manuscript. I staggered home.

I loved the job. I actually got paid to sit and read and then sit and write down my opinion. Synopses were easy for me. Thanks to Sister Mary Ligouri who believed that outlining *everything* including our English textbook would develop an orderly mind in even the most scattered student, I can synopsize anything in one page. This does not mean that my mind is orderly. It means that my mind can *appear* to be orderly when I need it to be, quite a different thing.

I make the distinction because my freelance reading career seemed to trigger some latent obsessive quality I didn't know I had. I read ten pieces of material the first week, eleven the next, fourteen the next, on and on. Soon I was staying up all night trying to beat my own record. For some reason, I thought this made sense until I shared my pride at my own record-busting with my therapist, and wet blanket that he was, he explained OCD. Oh rats, and I was having such a good time without the need to sleep or eat or communicate with other human beings! My therapist suggested I limit myself to ten pieces of material a week. I listened and did it because I'd heard the unspoken phrase "mental disorder" in what he was saying, then looked up OCD and decided that the warnings I'd heard in AA about "going to extremes, any extremes," were right on target. So I slowed down.

To replace the endorphins my record-busting had seemed to provide, I began playing around with my rejection letters.

Just in case any aspiring writers out there are becoming outraged, thinking "playing around!" What the hell does that mean? Let me say that most material is rejected not because it's not good. It's because it doesn't fit that particular company's/network's criteria for what they need at that time, the kind of material they do, and the deals they already have in place. That's why it's important for writers not to give up and to try, hard as it is, not to take rejection personally.

So, for the material I knew would not be accepted, I started writing satirical rejections. This not only slowed me down but also made me giggle to myself, an excellent fringe benefit in any job.

One day when I was returning material, synopsis and satire to the office, I ran into Marcy in the hall. "I've been reading your stuff," she said with *that* smile. "You're a funny writer."

She continued on down the hall while I stood rooted to the ground. *I'm a what?*

Sometimes, when a person you know to be honest and whose opinion you respect, labels you as something you've always wanted to be, unsolicited and out of the blue, your whole life spins around and takes another direction.

Buoyed by Marcy's unexpected comment, I drove home, one thought in my mind. "I'll write a book."

And I did. Over the course of the next many months, I wrote *The Cracker Factory*, my book about the psych ward, and finding AA.

The only thing I'd written prior to that was a short story about a jazz musician in New Orleans walking the streets on a rainy night contemplating suicide. Since I'm not a jazz musician and had never met one and had never been to New Orleans, the only thing I got right was the rain. It was a godawful story. I did my best to fix it by making it happen at night so I wouldn't have to describe the New Orleans I'd never seen, but still, it stunk big time. I tore it up.

When I was about halfway through, I asked Marcy if she'd read what I'd written so far. She said she would. The next time we had lunch she told me that she liked it a whole lot and would I mind if she shared it with her colleague, Marian Rees.

I'd met Marian, a sharp executive with a great sense of humor. The idea of Marian reading my stuff made me nervous. She had a reputation for having excellent taste in material. But I thought that if Marcy liked it, maybe Marian would, too, at least enough not to stop me in my tracks. At that point, muddling around in the middle of a manuscript uncertain of what I was doing, a truly negative response would have sent my book into the same wastepaper basket as my short story.

While Marian was reading the manuscript-in-progress, I contacted an agent who'd sent reams of material to the production company. The agent invited me to lunch where she told me that she never, *never, NEVER,* read material. She picked her writer clients based solely on her "gut instincts." And with that, she signed me up over tuna tar tare. Since it's difficult for a new writer to find an agent, I didn't care if she based her decisions on the I Ching. I later found out that the I Ching guided only her personal relationships. Her business advisor was Martine, a psychic she'd met on Stern's Wharf in Santa Barbara. She also had a personal assistant, her nephew Robert, whom she bullied and baited. With a crackerjack staff like that, she felt free to spend her days at spas while Robert sent material to every production company in town and Martine advised her long distance that the success spells she was casting for only $1500 a week were definitely working.

Now with a real live agent, sort of, I felt like a true professional.

Marian called and asked me to drop by her office the next time I was in the building. Trembling, I did. Marian was kind and oh, so encouraging. She said that she liked my writing and thought that the story was interesting. By any chance, was it autobiographical?

I hesitated. One of the traditions in AA is that we remain anonymous. Outside of AA, we're not supposed to say that we're *in* AA, though I'd told all my non-AA friends, including Marcy, and that was okay. But this felt different. Marian was not yet a close friend and she was a television executive. But she'd asked a yes or no question. A simple yes or no question. Only one of two answers was possible. "No" would be a lie. I said yes.

As it often does, my admitting to being an alcoholic led to a discussion of the disease. Marian was interested and receptive. She asked a lot of questions, particularly about women and alcoholism. The questions she asked made me think more deeply about what I was writing. My muddle cleared up. I went on.

Marcy continued to ask me how the book was "coming." My usual response was "like childbirth," long and painful. But her interest and encouragement kept me going. I couldn't imagine telling her that I'd stopped writing a book, even though most of the time, secretly, I wondered where I'd ever gotten the chutzpah to think I could be a writer in the first place. Not only was I a tad OCD, I was clearly delusional.

In one week, the first of three things happened: I finished the first draft of my book; then my agent announced she'd met a *"wonderful man, dahling,"* a real French nobleman named Henri which she pronounced "Hawn-weeee" and she was leaving for France immediately after the cocktail party she was throwing that weekend to introduce him to her clients; and third, Marian Rees went to New York on a business trip.

I met Henri, who was a French nobleman like I'm the Duke of Earl. I was polite to him as were the agent's other now-abandoned clients. Why we were polite I don't know except that writers when sober, tend to be more polite than dowagers and everyone was sober because the only "cocktails" our agent served were mimosas with ginger ale substituted for champagne.

On the same night, Marian Rees went to a much better party, where she sat at dinner next to a young book editor from Macmillan Publishing named Michael Denneny. In the course of dinner, Marian told him about *The Cracker Factory*, saying,

"You should read this manuscript."

Marian sent Michael the manuscript. He read it. He called me. He told me he was going to be in LA. Would I like to have lunch?

We had lunch at Musso & Frank Grill on Hollywood Boulevard. He asked me dozens of questions about myself. He told me he wanted to publish my book *but* he wanted my heroine to have children like I did. I told him that I'd left the kids out of the book because writing about being an alcoholic mom was too hard. I doubted I could do it. He said he was sure I could.

We were at lunch for five hours. After our turkey club sandwiches wore off, we ordered dinner. The waiters didn't seem surprised.

I left lunch/dinner promising Michael I'd *try* to write about being an alcoholic mom. "You'll do fine," he said cheerily. "Call me if you're having problems."

I had problems, most of them involving tears splashing on my typewriter keys. Not everything that came into my mind went into my book, it all came back. Every moment of the past I'd spent so much energy trying not to think about, was there like a movie running and running and I couldn't shut it off. I called Michael Denneny a lot. He told me that something so hard to do would ultimately make a difference. In what, he didn't say.

Marcy kept asking how the book was coming. Marian would ask what I'd heard from Michael. Michael would call to ask when the rewrite would be ready. Quitting because it was hard, was no longer an option.

I met Marcy through two writer husbands being introduced to each other by a third writer. I met Marian through my impromptu part-time job with Marcy. I met Michael through Marian's chance placement at a dinner party table.

Marcy Carsey, Marian Rees and Michael Denneny were the "deux ex machine" that never happens in fiction because it's not credible. Without them, particularly Marcy who spun me around, *The Cracker Factory* would never have been published.

From the bottom of my heart, thank you.

Before *The Cracker Factory* came out, Marcy called me. She'd recently changed jobs from the production company to the ABC television network. She told me that one of the problems inherent in networks working with the production companies was that television executives and writer/producers don't speak the same language. She thought that by hiring a couple of writers to act as liaisons, perhaps communication would improve. She asked me if I'd like to come to ABC as a Program Executive.

"What's that?" I asked.

"I'll show you when you get here," Marcy said.

"What if I don't like it?" I asked.

"You'll leave," she said.

"What if I'm no good at it?" I asked.

"I'll fire you," Marcy said.

That sounded reasonable to me. I told her I'd be at ABC in the morning to start the job. Where should I park?

Just like that, my accidental career in television began, and in my usual style. I didn't know where I was going or what I'd be doing once I got there. I just went.

And now, the last example of an accidental meeting. This one didn't lead to a job but to an adventure.

I met Susan through a friend who thought we should meet because we have the same birthday.

This reoccurring pattern of same birthdays is one I could never use in fiction because, again, it's incredible, meaning not believable. In real life and truth, this same pattern is just weird, strange and unfathomable, like so much of real life or at least in my life.

Susan is six feet tall and blonde with sharp blue eyes. Back in the day, she and Elvis Presley had been an item for almost a year. She told great stories about the early days, before Elvis was drafted and met Priscilla. They're Susan's stories, not mine, so I can't tell them.

Susan's interest and calling was metaphysics, primarily astrology. Her studies included the complicated math that's required to create astrological charts. She did the math without a computer, which to me is a feat comparable to walking through fire. As a math illiterate, I view mathematicians as shamans and gods, possessed of arcane knowledge and power.

Susan's knowledge of astrology intrigued me. Since there are few things that don't interest me, outside of reality shows and the tabloids, I'm also interested in people with a solid knowledge of their subject. Susan's knowledge was encyclopedic. I learned that there are charts for everything, but the one that intrigued me the most was the solar return chart. The idea behind the solar return (roughly) is that at the precise moment the sun returns to the astrological degree where it was when you were born, a special energy is unleashed. (It's the reason we light candles and make wishes on our birthday though few of us know that the origin of the tradition is astrological.) The idea captured me because it seemed to have a loose parallel in the Big Bang Theory, a single moment in space-time plus energy. As a fan of the old TV series and book, *Connections,* I thought that there might be something to it. As the beneficiary of an accidental life, my mind is always open to new ideas and the people who bring them.

When I asked Susan how it worked, she told me that our birthday would be the time to change our "vibe" for the coming year. All we had to do was go to a place where the energy was focused on what we wanted. (I do not understand how energy can focus on different areas of life in different places relative to a birth chart, so don't ask me. Ask an astrologer/math-shaman-goddess.)

For her part, Susan wanted an improvement in her business life. On my part, as always, I wanted to see "what happens next."

Susan went off to calculate the longitude and latitude where the "business energy" would be flowing at the moment of our solar return. She came back three days later with a map and a puzzled expression. "Here's the place but nobody ever goes there."

I looked at the map. Susan had circled a speck in French Polynesia, a tiny island a great distance from its nearest neighbor, Fiji. The speck was too small to be labeled on its face. But next to it, in the ocean, I read its name, Hoa Island.

"Wow, isn't this fascinating?"

Susan sniffed. "Not if we can't get there."

We got there. The trip involved flying to Fiji, staying overnight and then hiring a pilot who possessed both a rickety old plane and a desire to fly two American women to a place we were forbidden to go. Not that we knew that at the time. We knew nothing.

"You know nothing about this island," George had said, driving us to the airport. "The travel agents you called know nothing. The best they could do was tell you to call people in Fiji. The only thing you know is that this island exists. It could be a coral reef for all you know. You'll come back with your feet in shreds."

"It's only for three days," I said, pretending to sound reasonable.

"You don't know if there's a hotel or even people," George worried.

"A clerk at the Hilton in Fiji said she's pretty sure that a small plane can land there," Susan said cheerily.

"We're taking water, granola and sleeping bags," I reminded George. "We'll have everything we need."

Susan frowned. "I didn't think...we'll have to go in the bushes!"

"Three days," I repeated, convinced by my long-held theory that anyone can put up with anything for three days and considerably longer, for a real adventure.

"Three days is going to seem like forever," George complained. "I'll worry. You know I'll worry."

"Think of it as Woodstock, only far away," I advised. "If we weren't bringing our music, we'd be bored silly." I smiled at his profile. "Don't worry, Honey. Everything will be fine."

In Fiji at the Hilton, Susan stuffed her granola bag with small bottles from the minibar. "If I hate the island, I can pass out until the plane comes back."

"Thanks," I said, picturing Susan staggering over coral reef Hoa Island with bleeding feet, and me chasing her, trying to pour gin on her feet. "Wasn't this your idea?"

I could see that Susan was getting the collywobbles, so I did my best to encourage her. I certainly didn't want to land on this speck alone.

We had arranged for our pilot through a third party. When we arrived at the airport the next morning, we discovered that our pilot didn't speak English. He spoke a melodious, sensual French which we admired extravagantly but didn't understand.

And we were off, up into the clouds and over the ocean for a very long time. After a couple of hours, our pilot gestured at a picnic hamper, indicating we should open it. Inside, we found a perfect French lunch: bread and Brie and grapes, water for me and wine for Susan. I gulped all my water. Susan gulped all her wine. A half hour later we realized that the rickety plane had no facilities. By then the bushes Susan dreaded were beginning to look good. As time went on, even better. By the time the plane began its descent, our legs were crossed and we were holding our breath.

Then, as the final wispy clouds vanished and we could see the ground, we turned to each other, mouths hanging open. "Oh my God, look at that!"

The west end of the island was a military base surrounded by a high chain link fence. We could see the barracks, which from our height, looked like they were made of Legos. We saw tiny figures in uniform and the French flag flying over the barracks.

The pilot swooped the plane to the right and we saw the reason for the military installation: to the left of the barracks in its own separate installation, eighteen nuclear silos planted like trees were pointing straight up at the sky.

As we descended further, we saw the tiny figures in uniform become real soldiers with real guns.

The pilot landed as far as he could from the gates, opened the plane's door, yelled "Out, out, out!" and threw our bags onto the tarmac. As we scrambled down the ladder, we saw a jeep full of soldiers, including one who was pointing the front-mounted machine gun straight at us. They were all yelling and screaming at us.

The jeep and the gun were too much for Susan. "I've got to pee!" She yelled and bolted toward the barracks. I ran after her as fast as I could. As the jeep closed in and the plane took off, we burst into the barracks, startling a dozen or so military men and women working in what clearly was an office. Susan looked around wildly, spotted the universal skirted sign for "ladies room" and dashed in. I followed her. Right behind me were the dozen or so military. Right behind them, were the French MPs. Right behind them, was an irate officer shouting more loudly than anyone. Everyone shut up. The only sound was Susan flushing.

As Susan came out of the stall she grimaced at me. "Now what?"

I shrugged. "I don't know." I said the only thing I did know. "We don't speak French."

"So?"

"We need to know if anyone here speaks English."

I asked. Parlez-vous?

No one spoke English. On this secret military base on this secret atoll where they did secret things all day long, no one spoke the language of Bond, James Bond. Having read every Le Carre novel ever written, I was very surprised. How can you run a secret base efficiently without the ability to pick up coded messages in

Urdu? Or basic Russian?

When soldiers make hostile gestures with guns, it's not hard for them to convince two women to climb into a jeep. As we got in, I heard Susan mumble, "Why did I ever listen to me?"

We drove through the chain link gates and out into the residential area. The entire island could be walked from end to end and side to side, in an hour or so depending on how fast you walked. The rudimentary roads were dirt and narrow, lined on both sides with small wooden houses built on wood platforms to keep them above the ocean that sometimes rose over the roads.

The center of town was a church, a small school, a miniature post office, a grocery store and a jail. The French army took us to the jail.

Inside, the jail was rustic and picaresque like a jail in an old western movie. There was an old oak desk, a bench, some old chairs and a couple of cells with the doors hanging open. This reminded me of *Gunsmoke* where Matt Dillon would incarcerate drunks to sleep it off overnight but leave the cell doors open so they could haul their hungover asses out to find their own darn breakfast.

The French officer sat us down on the bench, then shouted at us. We got the general gist of the shouting. "Show him your passport, Susan."

We showed our passports. The officer shouted louder. "Smile at him, Susan."

"You're nuts. What am I smiling about? This asshole is scaring me."

The officer didn't react to "asshole" and neither did anyone else, so I figured that they really didn't understand English.

They fingerprinted and photographed us. "Now I can't ever go to France," Susan groaned. "They'll have a wanted poster with my face on it."

The next hour or so was taken up with the arrival of two more officers and urgent discussion among the three. We were tired and hungry but had stopped worrying about Susan's notion that they would shoot us and bury us under a silo and pretend we'd never arrived. Susan also read Le Carre.

Finally, a handsome young Polynesian man entered the jail, smiled at us and said, "'ello. I have English, a little."

The young man was the Hoa Island postmaster and so knew a smattering of English.

The officers gathered around. The postmaster said, "You here, why?"

A half hour earlier, I had whispered to Susan to let me talk. She whispered back. "Be my guest. We are both insane. It doesn't matter who talks."

I'd had an idea, not an original idea God forbid, but somebody else's great idea. A scene from a movie had popped into my head. It was a pivotal scene in *Close Encounters of the Third Kind* when Richard Dreyfus demands to know what all the military presence and subterfuge around Devil's Mountain is about. The brilliant Francois Truffaut responds with a beatific smile, "It is an 'Événement religieux'"– the English translation: a "Religious Experience."

I smiled at the postmaster. "We are on a spiritual journey." I crossed myself reverently and pointed upward at heaven.

The postmaster translated. The officers stared at us. The postmaster looked back at us and said, "Welcome."

Susan whispered, "Not bad." She crossed herself reverently, then batted her eyelashes piously, a gesture that seemed to confuse the French.

After that there was a lot of hurried discussion. A few minutes later, a young Polynesian woman appeared, at her side a young Polynesian man.

"My sister," the postmaster said. "Her spouse."

The jeep took us down the road to a very neat house where this smiling young couple gestured us inside. Once inside, we saw a living room with sparse but comfortable furniture, a shrine to the Virgin Mary and a tiny TV with rabbit ears. There were two small bedrooms. In one of them, a boy of about six was removing clothes and a few toys. The couple made us understand that we would be using the boy's room and he would be sleeping with them. Perpetually smiling, they gave us bottled water and food, unpeeled fruit, which was a very gracious gesture.

The postmaster arrived to tell us, in halting words and gestures, that the officers had sent him. There would be a military plane in three days. It would be flying to Fiji. We would be on that plane. We nodded. Three days! Perfect.

For the next three days, Susan and I received the most amazing hospitality I've ever experienced. People came to the house to welcome us in two languages, their native tongue and French. Our hostess whose name I heard as Budedee, walked us the length and breadth of the island, introducing us to every last soul who lived there. As we strolled along, a bored French soldier meandered along twenty steps behind, assigned to keep an eye on us. We felt sorry for him and offered him granola. He couldn't accept it but wanted to, we could tell.

Word had spread that the two foreign women were on a "spiritual journey." Because spirituality is important to them, the people of Hoa Island saw us as women on an important mission. During our visits, they asked us to hold their babies, an honor not lightly given and never given to outsiders.

I felt like a total and complete fraud until I realized that our journey did indeed contain a spiritual element, at least for Susan. And here I was reaping the benefit, feeling in absolute harmony with a group of great-hearted strangers.

One afternoon, out walking alone except for the guard, I ended up playing basketball with some schoolgirls, who cheered me on when I made a basket and giggled when I failed. I had a terrific time and went to get Susan. "Come play with us."

Susan said, "I want to go home." She looked tired, and continued, "I can't sleep with that damn ocean pounding all night."

"It lulls me to sleep," I admitted.

"We must have different rising signs," Susan said. "Yours likes oceans. Mine likes silence."

That night, I went to church with Budedee. I didn't know we were going to church when we left the neat little house. Budedee would smile at me, take my hand and sort of steer me where she wanted me to go.

Since most of the islanders had been converted to Catholicism by missionaries, this was a Catholic church complete with statues of saints. Unlike the dour presentation of my childhood parish, these plaster saints all had round brown faces and big welcoming smiles. They were so beautiful I wished I could take them home.

The service was also beautiful and different. It wasn't a Mass exactly or maybe it was but the format was more fluid. The priest spoke, then other people spoke, then there were hymns, lots of hymns, some of them sounding like chants. The service was a combination of two traditions, Catholic and Polynesian and very lovely to watch.

The next morning, Susan was perkier. While I was in church, the solar return moment had happened – the sun had returned to exactly nineteen degrees in our sign and Susan said she'd felt the energy. I thought I did, too, but couldn't be sure. At that exact moment, I'd been humming in church and inhaling some really fine sandalwood incense, all thoughts of solar return magic gone from my head.

Four French soldiers pulled up in the jeep to Budedee's front door. We hugged the family goodbye, hefted our duffles and got into the jeep. At the barracks, the shouting officer shouted at us some more. We heard the plane coming long before we could see it. It was an old WWII military plane that lumbered noisily through the sky, propellers straining.

Before we got on the plane, the officer directed a soldier to take our pictures again. We stood next to the plane, a medium sized brunette and towering blonde, smiling and waving at the camera like tourists, just for the hell of it. I told Susan, "I think that this picture goes to Interpol, Dangerous Whacko Division."

There weren't many people on the plane. Obviously, all of them were French and worked for the government. I whispered to Susan that we'd found the spies, "See that man in the trench coat?" I pointed. Susan squinted at the man in the trench coat. "He's got to be eighty at least."

"Devilishly good cover, what?" I whispered.

"Le Carre you're not." Susan shook her head. "And never will be."

After we landed in Fiji, we were approached by a tall man wearing the uniform of an English Army officer. He nodded politely. "Will you ladies please come with me?

We glanced at each other. By this time, we had our routine down pat. Do what's asked but say nothing.

We followed the man to a building and then up stairs and down hallways, down stairs and up hallways. Finally he showed us into a small room where an English officer sat behind a desk. He looked up at us; we were now sweaty and panting from hauling our heavy duffels for what seemed like miles in Fiji's thick humidity.

"You've been to Hoa Island?" he asked.

"Yes," I answered for both of us.

"How many silos did you see?"

I hesitated. Susan didn't think I'd ever be Le Carre? Ha, I'd show her. I could steal from Le Carre with the best of them.

"What silos? " I asked blandly, looking extremely puzzled.

He waved his ballpoint pen at us.

"Get out of here, Ladies." He went back to his work and we left, by now dragging our duffels behind us.

We landed at LAX and cleared customs. As we walked toward the outside door, two men in trench coats approached us.

The taller one said, "Do you mind if we look in your duffels?"

"Not at all," we said. We set our duffels on the floor. The men each dropped to one knee, opened them and searched through. They found leftover water, granola and used underwear. They zipped up the duffels and stood up. The taller one said, "Thank you."

They walked away quickly, disappearing into the crowd.

George picked us up. He opened the car door. "I'm so damned relieved that you're back. Did you have a nice time?"

"Well...."

Susan moved to San Francisco. I haven't heard from her in ages so I don't know if her business improved. Before she left, she confided that she'd never again make a solar return trip outside the United States. "My God, when I think of what could have happened to us!"

What happened to us was an adventure I never could have planned. I like to think that somewhere in a police vault in France, there's a photo of me with a question mark on it. "Who was this woman and why did she come unannounced to a secret military base where we house nuclear missiles?"

It makes me feel so Jason Bourne.

This story is true, every last detail, including the trench coats at LAX. It was ninety-seven degrees for God's sake! Had they just seen *Casablanca*?

Chapter 9.

(INT. MEETING ROOM)

Welcome to the Tuesday Night Women's Group of Alcoholics Anonymous.

I'm washing out the coffee pot because the last group that used this room didn't. I'm going to assume that they just forgot. If I start thinking that whoever the negligent pot washer was, just decided the next group could do it, I'll be blowing on the ember of a tiny resentment. Then immediately that ember will explode into a fire out of control and before I know it, I'll be snapping at everyone who comes through the door, none of whom knows the pot wasn't washed. Such is the nature of tiny resentments, the molehills we morph into mountains.

The pot's clean, the chairs are out and where's everyone? Like everyone else, I'm curious about Terri's friend, the circus performer. For some reason, I've been picturing her arriving in costume, straight from rehearsal.

Will she be spangly and in tights, a gorgeous aerialist, or maybe an equally gorgeous elephant rider, festive in bikini and feathered headdress?

While I'm trying to picture the new lady in a ringmaster's tuxedo, I hear footsteps approaching. I'm hoping it's Rachel, coming to make coffee.

It's not Rachel. I know I'm staring, but I can't help it. The lady standing beside the table, looking around, is an incredibly beautiful, incredibly talented movie star known on sight by everyone in the world.

I'm startled, of course. Our little group isn't in Beverly Hills, Brentwood or any other of the movie star haunts. We're in what's known as The Valley as in, "OMG, you *live* in the *Valley?*" Our neighbors aren't movie stars. Our neighbors shop at Target. In our old jeans and older rock and roll t-shirts. I say *we*. I mean *me*.

I put on my AA face which means a face that's friendly but doesn't indicate that I recognize her or might have an autograph book hidden under my sweater ready to wave in her face.

"Hi, I'm Cassie. Can I help you?"

She holds out her perfect hand and smiles with her perfect teeth, "Hi, I'm C. Is this a women's AA meeting?"

"Yes it is," I say, shaking hands. "Every Tuesday evening."

She smiles. "Oh, good." She gestures vaguely at the door. "I'm working down near City Hall. I just wrapped for the night. I carry my meeting directory with me. I saw that there's a women's meeting here tonight, so I thought I'd come over."

"Welcome," I say. "I'm just waiting for everyone else to arrive. We're a small group. Sometimes everyone walks in the door together."

"Sounds friendly." C. smiles. "Where's the coffee? I haven't had a cup since lunch. I live on the stuff."

Yikes! Am I a bad hostess or what?

"Rachel is our coffee maker. She isn't here yet," I explain. Then in the interest of honesty, I added, "I make terrible coffee. Battery acid. Undrinkable. That's why I'm waiting for Rachel."

C. laughed. "My mother made coffee that ate holes in the tablecloth. I make great coffee. Where's the pot?"

I show her the pot. In a second, she's adding both coffee and water without even measuring. I watch, admiring her talent and confidence.

From behind me I hear Katherine and Rachel. "Excuse me," I say to C., then hurry off to Katherine and Rachel.

Rachel is staring at C.'s back. "Who's that making coffee?"

I tell her. Rachel gapes. "You're kidding!"

"No. She's been filming something at City Hall and wanted to come to a meeting. Let's just all be cool, okay?"

Katherine squints. "Is that Cameron Diaz?"

"No Katherine, she's not," I say, then beg, "Please lower your voice."

Katherine persists. "Is she that *Grey's Anatomy* girl who almost died and makes racy movies?"

"No," Rachel tells her. "You're thinking of Katherine Heigl."

Katherine glowers. "Then I don't know who she is so I don't have to be cool."

"Please Katherine," I ask, "Don't ask her any personal questions including her last name."

Katherine looks at me with honest amazement. "Why would I ask her personal questions? That would be rude."

I nod. "You're right, Katherine. We're never rude."

"And don't forget it," Katherine says. "Courtesy is a hallmark of civilization. Now get away from my chair so I can sit down."

Katherine sits heavily. Rachel spots Leslie, Terri and her friend, and Elena without her baby coming in the door and hurries to meet them. No doubt Rachel's bursting to tell them about our visitor and deliver today's message: be cool.

I hear the buzzing at the doorway as the women react to the news. I notice that Terri's friend, a tall but slightly built, freckled girl, is wearing jeans instead of spangles. She looks more like a high school senior than a circus performer, you know, the "cute" senior with the shy smile.

Everyone is putting on their "cool" faces except Terri who is blatantly staring at C.'s back.

"Let's begin," I call briskly. I feel like Sister Mary David who would begin every assembly with a shout and sharp clap of her hands, as though she was facing a mob of volatile gangbangers instead of two hundred sullen, beaten-down Catholic high school girls.

Everyone sits at the table including C. who smiles and says "hi" to everyone.

I skip over the group business, not because of our guest but because we don't have any new business tonight. Last week we talked about the upcoming AA convention in Bakersfield and next week we'll talk about our annual group potluck, but tonight there's no news.

I ask Terri to read Chapter Five, hoping the task will get her head back into the meeting. If she stares any harder at C. her eyeballs will fall out onto the table.

Terri reads Chapter Five, *How It Works*, at first breathlessly, then in her normal semi-bored tone. She finishes.

I look around the table. "Rachel?"

Rachel looks startled. "Me?"

"You can skip if you want," I remind her, picturing the first AA meeting in history where no one says anything.

Rachel

(to Cassie)

No, no. I'm happy to share.

(deep breath)

My husband Stan and I are planning a vacation. The kids want to go to Disney World in Florida which is making me crazy because we have Disneyland right here in LA and they've been a million times and I'll be damned if I know why LA people go to Orlando it's so damned humid and I'm Rachel, alcoholic and damned happy to be here sober, that's all.

>(pause)

Thank you.

Cassie

Thank *you*.

>(then)

Katherine?

Katherine

I'm Katherine, alcoholic and I'm so grateful for this group I can't tell you.

>(leaning toward C.)

You're new here Honey but let me tell you, these girls are the best. I felt so lousy all the time, I was going to stop coming to meetings....

>(looks around at group)

I know. You girls didn't know that but it's true. It was getting too much to get up and get ready.

>(to C.)

Anyway, the girls took me to a doctor who got me tuned up. Now I can ride the bus. And I look forward to meetings. Before, I was only scared to miss them. My apartment's next door to a liquor store that delivers. How's that for living dangerously, huh?

>(then)

Thank you, Girls. That's all.

Cassie

If you'd stopped coming, we'd have been all over you, Katherine. You're not getting away that easily.

(then)

I've been to meetings in people's living rooms, bedrooms and sickrooms. You don't have to be mobile to be in AA. *Have Sobriety, Will Travel.*

Katherine

I should have known. You girls are so nosey.

(smiles)

At least I won't be one of those old ladies who dies alone and nobody finds her and her cat eats her feet.

Rachel

For God's sake, Katherine!

Katherine

(calmly)

It happens.

Cassie

(quickly)

Elena?

Elena

(low voice)

My husband didn't come home this morning.
My friend is looking for him. The baby is with
my neighbor. That's all.

(then)

Oh, I'm Elena, grateful alcoholic.

Around the table, buzzing rises.

Cassie

Are you okay, Elena? Have you called the
police?

Elena

No.

Katherine

Why not?

Big round tears roll down Elena's cheeks. Rachel slips her
arm around Elena's shoulders.

Elena

I think he ran off with a woman from his
work. I know he was seeing her. Sometimes
he doesn't come home from work until noon,
and he smells really funky.

Rachel

(angry)

I'd kill the son of a bitch!

Cassie

(quickly)

Elena doesn't want to do that, Rachel. Prisons don't have day care.

(to Elena)

Has he been gone for twenty-four hours?

Elena nods.

Leslie

You can call the police and report him missing.

Elena

He's not missing. He's with some cunt.

(quickly)

Excuse me. I don't use that word.

Cassie

It's okay. You're angry. And worried. Maybe most of all, you're worried.

Elena

I don't drink. I work. I take care of the baby.

And he runs off on me?

(furious)

Is this what I get for staying sober?

Cassie

What you get for staying sober is sobriety. You know that, Elena.

(then)

Drinking was wrecking your life. You couldn't stop. You wanted to stop. You came here. You stopped drinking.

(smiles)

AA doesn't guarantee that our lives will be perfect. Only that sober, we'll be able to handle whatever comes.

Rachel

And we'll still make mistakes. But we won't make excuses.

(then, quietly)

Are you using your husband's…whatever this is…as an excuse for a slip?

Elena

No! How dare you!

Rachel

Then where's Lucy ?

(quietly)

It's easier to stop off at a bar on the way home when a neighbor is watching the baby, isn't it?

Elena looks down at her hands. The tears we were all expecting well up in her eyes. Leslie, who's sitting beside Elena, rubs her shoulder.

Rachel

Been there, done that, Elena. If a slip worked...if it made you feel any better...I'd tell you.

(laughs)

Hell, I'd probably join you.

(then)

But it doesn't.

Cassie

Rachel's right. In forty years I've never heard anyone who had a slip and came back, say that their slip was anything but a nightmare.

C.

So many don't come back. They stay out there, way out there. They lose everything that's important to them. Then they just disappear.

(then)

Oh, I'm C., very grateful alcoholic.

We all turn to look at C., even Elena. We're not surprised that she spoke. We're surprised that she sounds so…normal…like any one of us. Maybe we were expecting that a movie star would speak in Shakespeare or maybe tongues. Or more likely, given the times, MRV (mall rat vapid), our local dialect. But *normal*? Who wouldda thunk it?

Elena

(softly)

Okay. You're right. I was thinking about drinking…or getting ready to think about drinking…I'm just so upset.

(then)

What'll I do if he doesn't come back?

Cassie

One day at a time, Elena. You'll figure it out.

Rachel

You're not alone, you know. You have us. We'll help you.

Cassie

But you've got to stay sober. Take that first drink and after that, alcohol makes all your choices for you.

Rachel

It's like Cassie's sponsor said – if you get drunk, tear up my phone number.

C.

(appalled, bursts out)

What?

Rachel

(indicating Cassie)

She's been sober longer than I've been alive.
Her sponsor must have been right.

Cassie

Alice was right for herself and right for me.
That doesn't mean she was right for everyone.
Or even *anyone* else.

C.

I don't hang up on people who are drunk
when they call me.

(thinks about it)

Come to think of it, I do screen calls. Who
can listen to drunks all day long?

Leslie

Back to Elena.

(then)

Think ahead, Elena. Do you want to lose your
daughter?

Elena gasps.

Elena

My God, no!

Leslie

If you're drinking, sooner or later someone, a
neighbor, a relative, someone, will call social
services.

> (then firmly)

If that happens, don't ask me to be your lawyer.
I can't stand addict moms who think they have a
right to their kids. They don't. Neither would
you.

Elena stares at Leslie, horrified.

Leslie

When it comes to addicts and kids, I pick the
kids. So do you, Elena. Right?

Elena doesn't answer. Leslie leans forward.

Leslie

Drinking or Lucy. Which do you pick?

Elena

> (softly)

Lucy.

Leslie

Good. After the meeting I'll drive you to the
police station. No matter how mad you are,
your husband is still missing. You need to file
a report. Okay?

Elena

　　(nodding)

Okay. Thank you.

Cassie

Feel any better, Elena?

Elena

I'm not going to drink, if that's what you
mean.

Cassie

That's what I mean. Good.

Terri

Me next!

Cassie

Terrific. Go!

Terri

I'm Terri and I'm hardly ever grateful. But I'm not drinking, so I'm good.

(smiling at friend)

This is my friend, Lynn. We were at the same foster home in fifth grade. Lynn was the house clown. Now she's a real clown in the circus. She wears orange hair and a red nose and tumbles. Say hello.

Everybody

Hello, Lynn.

Lynn nods and smiles. She seems far too shy to be a clown but we know better. We've all worn our masks in the past. Some of us have worn so many masks for so long we come to AA with more personalities than Sybil. We can only hope that with the help of the program, the personalities we discard are the right ones, the Bad and the Ugly, not the Good.

Terri

(continuing)

Lynn wanted to come with me tonight. I've been telling her about AA. She thinks she's been drinking too much. She wants to….

Cassie

(interrupting)

Excuse me, Terri. Maybe Lynn would like to tell her own story?

Terri

    (immediately)

Oh yeah, right.

    (to Lynn)

Tell 'em.

Lynn

    (hesitates, then)

Uh…it's like Terri says. I'm a clown but I want
to be an acrobat.

    (then, determined)

I'm *going* to be an acrobat. You gotta think
positive. You got to like see it in your head
before you can do it. You got to like *visualize*.
Athletes do that. They go over every move in
their heads and this is too weird, but their
muscles like start firing. Just from *visualizing*.

Terri

    (interrupting softly)

Lynnie?

Lynn stops and looks at Terri. She seems confused.

Lynn

Where was I?

Terri

You want to talk about drinking.

Lynn

That's right. Thanks, Terri.

> (then, to the group)

Some people in the circus drink a lot. Some drink all the time. Some only drink after the show. Sometimes a bunch of us go out to eat. I usually have a cheeseburger but sometimes I also have a beer.

> (then)

What should I do?

We all looked at each other including C. who, faced with this group newcomer puzzle, isn't quite certain how to respond. AA doesn't diagnose. All that's required for AA membership is a desire to stop drinking. There's no protocol for how much, how long and what you drank. Nobody asks. But Lynn is asking us. No one comes to AA without a reason.

Cassie

Why do you think you have a drinking problem, Lynn?

Lynn

Because I read this thing in a magazine – it was Scientific Monthly – I found it on a bus – it said problems with booze are genetic, like they run in families. A social worker told me my mom was like a drunk. I never met her in person but the social worker did. She was double-jointed, my mom I mean.

Cassie

The article was right about genetics. And choosing not to drink is always an option, whether or not you have a problem.

(then)

Lots of people with alcoholic parents decide they don't want to drink.

Katherine

(not getting it)

You've had what? Ten beers in your life? Maybe you just worry too much.

Cassie

That's for Lynn to say, Katherine. When I came to AA, people told me I was too young to be an alcoholic. I could have died waiting to be old enough.

(to Lynn)

Is there another reason that drinking worries you, Lynn?

Lynn

I don't drink very often but when I have just one beer....

(sighs)

I get so confused. It's like my head doesn't work. It just stops. I don't know what to do next. I have to ask somebody if it's time to go home. And where home is.

We all look at each other. Leslie, who's been listening intently, asks a question in her subtle, lawyer-like fashion.

Leslie

Have you ever been hit in the head?

Lynn

(confused)

Yes. No. I fall down a lot. Practicing. My goal is the Cirque du Soleil.

Terri

(excited for Lynn)

Lynnie has goals!

Katherine

More likely she has a concussion.

(to Lynn)

Sweetheart, you think falling down is hard now? Just wait 'til you trip in your walker. You fall down and the damn thing falls on you like a damn metal ladder. It's crash, clunk and help, I can't get up!

Rachel

(to Lynn)

My grandma was like you. One glass of wine and she was three sheets to the wind! She'd dance like a loon, spin, spin, spin. Grandpa would go hide in the basement.

Confused, Lynn looks around the table.

Lynn

Are you saying I don't drink enough or that I drink like an old lady?

Cassie

(quickly)

Neither, Lynn.

(then)

Some people have no tolerance for alcohol. None. Zero. One whiff and they're gone. It's like an allergic reaction.

Terri

(remembering)

The Book says that alcoholism is an allergy of the body combined with an obsession of the mind.

Cassie

In 1935, the disease concept was a very advanced idea. Before that, people thought that alcoholism was a sin, like eating meat on Friday.

(then, to Lynn)

We have another definition: "If alcohol is adversely affecting any part of your life, then you have a problem with alcohol."

Terri

(getting it)

It's affecting Lynn's goals!

Lynn

(getting it, too)

And finding my way home.

Cassie

Then your body has a zero tolerance for alcohol. It happens.

Rachel

(to Lynn)

When you go out, is it hard to pass on the beer?

Lynn

(shrugging)

I don't care one way or the other. I like Dr. Pepper better.

We all look at each other. Oh, don't we wish!

Rachel

Just stick with soda. You'll be fine.

Lynn

That's a relief! I'm glad I came here tonight.
You guys know everything.

Terri

See Lynnie, I told you! You need to hang out
with AAs.

Leslie

    (to Lynn)

Do you have a computer?

Lynn

Not me personally but I can use one whenever....

    (then)

Why?

Leslie

There are online AA women's meetings and
chat rooms. I have website addresses I'll give
to you.

Terri

    (excited)

You can stay connected on the road.
Awesome.

Katherine

Why didn't I know about this? I can stay home and go to a meeting.

Cassie

(to Katherine)

Don't you dare. We'd miss you.

Katherine

(sighing)

The spirit is willing, but....

Leslie

(to Lynn)

In online AA, members call group meetings "f2f" – face to face. They go when they can.

Cassie

Just stay in touch!

(then)

We'll give you our phone numbers. Call anytime. Collect if you need to.

Lynn

(surprised)

Your own home personal numbers?

Cassie

Sure.

Lynn looks like we've given her a present. We realize that outside of the insular world of the circus, she has no friends. Since before that she had no family, Lynn's spent most of her life in solitary.

Lynn

Awesome.

(happy)

Now I'll know what to say when my friends are all buying beer. I'm allergic!

Katherine

And wear a helmet when you're tumbling, please, Sweetheart?

(whispers to Joyce)

The child needs a mother.

Lynn

(overhearing)

I had a mother. She left me at the Airport Hilton in Denver. I don't want no more mothers.

Cassie

I don't either, Lynn, but we all need friends.

Terri

>(to Lynn)

Now you have a whole bunch.

I look at my watch. As usual, I'm late.

Cassie

Coffee break, ladies.

C H A P T E R   T E N

WRITERS OF FICTION DEVELOP A KNACK FOR STANDING IN the shoes of their characters and looking out at the world through the characters' eyes.

So do alcoholics. When the newcomer arrives, we know her story, not the pertinent details that make her an individual, but in general. We know that she did not plan to become an alcoholic. It was never her goal, her dream, or the accomplishment she wanted first on her resume. To paraphrase the old saying "alcoholism happened while she was making other plans." It affected her life, then consumed her life. She had many losses. Finally she decided that she needed some help. One of the places she looked was AA. She went to a meeting. Something that she heard at her first or her twelfth or her fortieth meeting struck a chord deep inside her. She knew that she was in the right place. Now, with or without other therapies and help, she's a member of AA. She has a home group. She's sober. The alcoholic behaviors that led to her loss of family, friends and jobs, eventually subside. She feels better. That's everyone's story. We all know a good part of the story the moment we say welcome to the newcomer. We all come to the table viewing our own and others' lives through the singular perspective of an alcoholic.

As they say, "takes one to know one." And the "one" we know, is the same as the one we see in the mirror.

That's how women and men of wildly diverse backgrounds, ages, strata of society and warring political views can walk into a new meeting anywhere in the world and be welcomed immediately as "one of us."

In case you were wondering.

Chapter 11.

(INT. MEETING ROOM)

It's been a few minutes since I called for the coffee break. Everyone has coffee but is ignoring my Whole Foods cookies, the fat-free, sugar-free, gluten-free vanilla pinwheels they all hate. Sure they taste like hubcaps but they're healthy. No, I don't think that we'll live forever but Katherine and I would like another twelve minutes of vibrant old-timer life. We have bitches we haven't yet bitched and moans we haven't yet moaned. Only kidding. We're grateful as all get out. If we hadn't stopped drinking Katherine and I would be In Memoriam, not as much fun as Here and Now.

Speaking of Katherine, she's asleep with her head on the table. When coffee break is over she'll wake up, alert and feisty as ever. I've never understood why it takes us humans so long to discover the glory of Cat Naps. A few minutes out-cold transforms into hours-alert. The young'uns should try it. Cat Naps beat meth for energy any day and you don't get arrested and your house doesn't blow up. Cat Naps are a good thing, as Martha would say.

Leslie is copying online AA websites for Lynn, with Terri looking over her shoulder. I can already see Terri glued to her computer, chatting online to her Sober Sisters night and day. I'll have to remind her of Moderation and f2f meetings or we'll never see her.

Rachel is sitting at an empty table with her arm around Elena. When I look at them I feel Rachel's warm heart reaching out to Elena and Elena's grief losing its grip. Women are so good at this.

What do the men do, I wonder? I've never been to a men's meeting of course. But I know because I'm human and have a brother and I like men, that their grief cuts just as deeply as ours. When there are no women around how do they comfort each other? I'll ask my brother.

I'll ask my sister, too. She, like me, has always worked with men. She's a lawyer, a damned fine lawyer as well as a damned fine sister. She's also an insightful person who married one of the world's really good guys and raised two sons and a daughter. She'll know.

The men I've worked with never showed grief. They manned up. They machoed. They drank. They did drugs. They had heart attacks. They left their wives for lap dancers. But show grief? Are you crazy? That would be unmanly.

C.'s standing alone, staring into space. Her lips are moving. Since I've worked with actors I know that she's in her own world, doing one of two things: memorizing lines or rehearsing. Still, no newcomer should ever stand alone at a meeting. Sometimes a friendly, "Hi, how's it going?" to a newcomer is the difference between that newcomer returning for a second meeting or feeling unwelcome and never coming back.

Some newcomers respond to the "hi" with hissing and spitting like feral cats. They want to be left alone until they feel comfortable in this new and admittedly different place. That's fine. It takes all kinds. We have all kinds. The friendly "hi" is never wrong.

In this case, since I don't know if C. is a newcomer to AA or just to this group, the "hi" is especially important.

Cassie

Hi. How's it going?

C. is momentarily startled, forced to make a too-abrupt return from her other world to this one. Right now she has one foot in each. She's the proverbial deer caught in my headlight.

C.

Too bad Jesus Christ was illiterate.

>   (then, adamant)

I don't want to read what people thought
about him thirty years after he died. I want to
know what *he thought,* and what *he felt.* I want
to read his diary.

Okay. I can figure this out.

Cassie

You mean *The Autobiography of Jesus Christ* BY
Jesus Christ.

C.

Exactly!

>   (then)

I'm sure those other guys did the best they
could...the Gospel writers...but they wrote
about Jesus a long time after he was gone
and...who knows what they got right? They
said he did this and said that, but were they
right?

>   (anxious)

Can you remember what everybody said at a
dinner party you went to thirty years ago?

Cassie

I can't remember *last year's* Thanksgiving
dinner!

C.

(excited)

<u>That's</u> what I mean!

(then)

Some of the stories were written by people
who never even knew Jesus! I could write a
book about Charlie Chaplin because I've met
people who knew him but none of the stories
would be accurate. I'd be writing my opinion
of City Lights, not the truth about Chaplin.

(sighs)

Of course Mohammed wasn't literate either
but he came from an oral tradition. Who
knows about Moses. If he was educated in the
palace of the Pharaoh, then he must have read
hieroglyphics.

Then there's the Ten Commandments...wow...
a finger of fire etching stone tablets! Now *that's*
a great visual! Someday I'm going to direct.

I'm listening and wondering if C.... is still stuck in her
other world or if maybe, I hope not, she's whacked. She sees my
puzzled look. She laughs.

C.

(continuing)

I'm not nuts! I'm researching the Bible. I'm
playing yet another version of poor old Mary
Magdalene. This one's the hooker with the
heart of gold archetype. Lots of fake hair, kohl
eyes and weeping.

(shaking her head)

I love research. I dig and dig. But what am I
playing? Sinner? Saint? Mother? Wife? My
head's gonna explode.

(shrugging)

All because Jesus didn't write it down.

Cassie

Aggravating.

C.

More than aggravating. Incomprehensible.

(smiles)

Nice meeting you have here. Nice women.
Sweet of you to pretend you don't recognize
me.

Cassie

Everyone's entitled to their privacy.

C.

(sighs)

The only place I can get it is in a women's
group. I was in Neiman's ladies room one day
and the woman in the stall next to me shoved
her cell phone under the partition and took
my picture. While I was peeing.

Cassie

That's awful.

C.

Par for the goddamned course.

>   (eyes the cookie plate)

I'd love to have one of those but I don't dare.
I'm right on the cusp of chub.

Cassie

Fat-free, gluten-free, sugar-free.

C.

Hot Damn!

While C. grabs a handful of hubcaps, I glance at my watch.

Cassie

>   (calling)

Coffee break's over.

Like magic, Katherine wakes up. Everyone returns to the table. I sit down next to C., who's gobbling cookies like they're her last meal. I know that everyone wants to hear her share but, benevolent dictator that I am, I decide to let her eat in peace.

Cassie

Leslie?

Leslie's head comes up sharply. She looks surprised.

Leslie

Me?

> (then)

Sure.

> (then)

First of all, I'm so grateful that I can do something to help Elena. If I wasn't a lawyer I wouldn't know what forms to fill out at the police station. I wouldn't know what Elena should say. And just as importantly, what she shouldn't say. If she goes in alone and just rambles on, they might think she's trying to divert suspicion.

Elena

Suspicion? Of what?

Leslie

Some people kill their spouses and then report them missing. Look at Scott Peterson.

Rachel

YOU look at him. He's disgusting.

Elena

> (frightened)

The police are going to think I killed my husband?

Leslie

No, I'll be with you! I won't let that happen!

Cassie

Won't it look suspicious if Elena comes in with a lawyer?

Leslie

I'm not going as a lawyer. I'm going as a friend.

(then)

An informed friend, true, but a friend.

Cassie

Maybe Elena should have *two* friends.

Leslie

You're not a lawyer.

Cassie

Even better.

C.

Sonja Sotomayor was inspired to become a lawyer by watching *Perry Mason*. I only played one and I read *real* law books.

Leslie

(to C.)

I guarantee you Sonja's read real law books since.

Cassie

(to Leslie)

Leslie, you were sharing....

Leslie

Right.

(then)

Anyway, I'm grateful to serve. And grateful for this group. And grateful that I don't have to drink anymore. And....

Elena

(interrupting)

I'm not going to the police station.

Leslie

Yes, you are.

Elena

It's nothing but a hassle. The bitch can have him.

Leslie

You don't even know if there is a bitch.

Elena

(wisely)

There's *always* a bitch.

Rachel

Your guy screws around?

Elena

Never!

Leslie

(frustrated)

Elena!

Cassie

(interrupting)

Please, Leslie. Share.

Leslie

Okay. Where was I?

(pauses, then nods)

Right. I was being grateful.

(then)

I'm grateful for everything in the whole
stinking universe except I might be just a tiny
bit resentful about one tiny thing.

Leslie looks down the table at C., measures her words.

Leslie

Most of you know that I have a...friend. Well,
my friend made an...appointment...with me.
He was supposed to come over night before
last. He didn't show up. He didn't call either.
He didn't answer his cell.

(then)

I started thinking maybe something happened
to him. Like an automobile accident. Or heart
attack. Or maybe his wife died.

Katherine

(whispers to Cassie)

Pity the fool.

Leslie

So I went to his office.

Everyone gasps.

Leslie

(very defensive)

It's okay. We're colleagues. I told his assistant

that I was there to discuss a case.

(makes a face)

The twit told me that I wasn't on David's
books.

(angry)

Not on David's books! What the hell does she
know! I'm on David's books like she wouldn't
believe! Her toes would curl!

(deep breath)

She made me wait forever. When I finally got
into David's office, he apologized like...crazy.
I mean, he almost cried. He told me that one
of his cases had gotten off-track. He'd been
totally immersed. He forgot our date.

(then)

I know how that is, do I ever! I've pulled
those all-nighters. I've lost track of time. I've
forgotten to eat. I've forgotten to return calls
and...

(fighting back tears)

...he forgot *me*....

(then)

But I understand. I do, except...I wish he'd
left his cell on...if I'd just heard his voice I
wouldn't have worried.

(straightens, puts on lawyer face)

So I have a tiny resentment but I'll get over it.

(quickly)

When his case is over he'll call me.

Katherine

You ever heard the term kiss-off?

Leslie

    (coldly)

I've read my share of Raymond Chandler.

    (staring, daring her)

Why, Katherine?

Cassie

    (quickly)

C., would you like to share?

C.

Glad to.

    (smiles)

My name's C. and I'm a recovering
alcoholic/addict though more addict
than alcoholic.

    (then)

AA groups are like Forest Gump's box of
chocolates. You never know what you're going
to get. Besides sobriety, I mean. You always get
sobriety. I like this group. Reminds me of my
mom's kitchen in Pittsburg.

    (smiles)

My name's not C., it's Marsha.

I'm five years older than you think. I left my

heart back home and my real nose in Beverly Hills.

(then)

About nine years ago I was taking riding lessons, trying to "round out" the old resume. Anything you can do that will impress producers...ride, snorkel, skydive, do open heart surgery...helps get the next job.

(then)

The horse threw me. I used to call the poor horse a damned skittish nag but it was me who was skittish. I made the horse nervous. He bolted. I broke my back.

(then)

Do you know how easy it is to get painkillers? And sleeping pills when the painkillers keep you awake? And pills for anxiety because you know that the pain's coming back? And pills so you can get up in the morning and go to work without a back brace? And more pills because the same old pain pills aren't working anymore.

And then you're lying in bed high all day just watching the Food Channel until you notice it's dark out and you've run out of pills. And, you've also run out of friends to go get the pills. So you start paying people to go to the drugstore. Creepy people who were stealing my stuff. To pay for their own drugs. I let them steal from me. I needed them. I needed the drugs.

(then)

Then when your real doc cuts you off, you find other docs, the not-so-particular. You pay

them, you own them. They write you scripts
in different names. The creepy people pick
them up.

    (then)

I got addicted. I didn't mean to but…you all
know how it is. Once you stop taking meds as
directed, it's all down hill puke and pink
elephants from there. At the end I was paying
nine docs and a pharmacist.

    (then)

I went to rehab. Not one of those fifty thou-
sand a month spa places…never understood
why an addict who can't see straight or hold
down soup needs marble statues and a heated
pool…I went home and checked into a
hospital. Then an AA angel arrived and…here
I am.

    (then)

I take full responsibility, but…I wish doctors
would keep up their end of the bargain.
There's a quack looking for a buck on every
corner but they'll sue if you call them drug
dealers.

    (looking around)

I'm sure I'm not the only one here who's had a
prescription drug problem.

Everyone nods. Though none of us that I know of has had
that experience, we know what she means. We meet more and
more people in other groups with prescription drug problems.

Katherine

It's all better living through chemistry, Honey.

Terri

Some kids will take anything in the medicine
cabinet. Not just pain pills but antibiotics and
birth control…anything that looks like a pill.

Rachel

Boys are taking birth control?

Terri

They don't ask. They just take.

Rachel

Just wait till they start growing boobs.

Katherine

No. Boys *must* read the label. They *can't* be
that dumb.

Terri

They believe girls who tell them that they're
on the pill. How dumb is that?

Katherine

(sighing)

I've lived too long.

(looking up to heaven)

Just joking.

Cassie

(to C.)

Thank you for sharing, Marsha.

C.

You're welcome.

(then)

Just so you know. The withdrawal from prescription drugs was so much more painful than my bad back and lasted so long…it was….

(then)

Picture this. You're shaking and sweating and retching and three burley men are beating you up with clubs.

Katherine

Those men visit my house every morning.

(quickly)

I don't shake and retch. I take only Advil. I'm fine by noon.

C.

Good for you.

(then)

I'm just saying…beware. We have to be vigilant.

Cassie

We have to take as directed. Like grownups.

Katherine

You've said that before.

Cassie

I'm saying it again. We *grow* in sobriety.
We're not teenaged boys, swallowing estrogen.
We're adults.

Terri

Except me.

Lynn

And me.

Cassie

Keep coming back. We'll help you grow up.
AA has no age requirement.

Katherine

I'm going to die at this table.

(looking up to heaven)

Not now. Please?

Cassie

Elena, will you read *A Vision for You*?

Elena reads the lovely essay *A Vision for You*, finishing with:

Elena

...please join us as we trudge the happy road to destiny.

(smiles)

Trudge...trudge...trudge...I used to hate that word. Trudge sounds so hard and boring like you're marching in the mud to nowhere....

(then)

But I like it now. Trudge means I don't have to hurry.

Terri

And it says that the road is happy.

Rachel

It works if you work it.

Cassie

After a moment's silence we'll join hands and say the Serenity. Then Leslie and I will take Elena to the police station.

Elena

I said I'm not going.

Cassie

Right now you don't know why your husband

is missing. You don't have the info to know if
this is something you have to accept or a situation you'll need the courage to change. This
could be a chance to work your program.

Elena

Oh shit, that makes sense.

Cassie

But only if you want to.

Elena

Cut the crap, Cassie. You got me.

I smile to myself. Thank you, Alice, for all the times you "got"
me.

CHAPTER TWELVE

My job title at ABC Television was Program Executive. Since all businesses are male created and dominated, titles are of utmost importance. They must be spit-polished and adorned with gold braid. They must be puffed up to the edge of bursting and draped with neon laurel leaves. Otherwise the male bearers of said titles deflate to a point beyond the help of even Viagra.

In the real world the title, Program Executive, translates into Glorified Messenger. I was assigned to Current Comedy which means the sitcoms already in production. Every week I read the scripts for four sitcoms, *Welcome Back Kotter, What's Happening!, Barney Miller,* and *Fish,* plus scripts for pilots in production which might someday be scheduled.

I would type up my thoughts about these scripts, their stories, comedic values, character arcs and general worthiness on one page, then send that page to everyone in the company even vaguely associated with comedy, soliciting their comments, questions, approval and/or scorn.

Writing up these one-pagers made me sweat. Even though I was already a real writer, writing a novel is different from writing a sitcom. It's the difference between tennis and golf. They're both sports, but just because you're Venus Williams on Tuesday doesn't mean you can be Tiger Woods on Wednesday. I'd never written a sitcom. I had no clue how to do it. With a gun to my head, I couldn't have written a sitcom (later, I learned from experts willing to teach me and loved the process). But there I was, a bona fide network executive whose job it was to foist upon professional sitcom writers/producers my uninformed opinion on what they do best. Oh the hubris of it all! And I knew it.

I introduced myself to Danny Arnold, the volatile genius behind *Barney Miller* this way: "My name is Joyce Burditt. I'm your new program exec. I think that *Barney Miller* is brilliant. I don't know anything about sitcoms so I'll just sit over here and watch what you do."

Danny's eyes widened. He grinned. "Will you marry me?"

I sat and watched for a couple of hours before I delivered the message my ABC execs had given to me, "ABC would like you to do *this...this...and this...."*

Danny nodded, not agreeing but playing his part. "I would like ABC to do *this...this...and this.*" He took the one-pager I handed him and didn't even tear it up, unlike some other producers who, insulted by network messages, threatened to tear me up along with my "notes." They didn't mean it, of course. They were simply bemused by the notion that television execs, notorious for their lack of creativity, could separate good story ideas from bad ones better than the writers who wrote and produced them.

So, that's how it went. All day every day, I delivered my notes and other messages. Often, I delivered messages that *nobody* wanted to hear. The network would ask the producer to do something and the producer's answer would be "no." Or the producer would ask the network for something and the Great Network Voice in the Sky would boom, "Not in this lifetime!"

On those days, my messages were greeted with frowns and occasionally (surprise!) profanity. Then my job became a duplicate of childhood days when my parents weren't speaking to each other and it was my task to relay their less-than-cordial communications. Then the network was my father, "Do this right now!" And the producers were my mother, "You tell that son of a bitch...."

I was good at this part of the job because I'd already done it.

Also, I liked everybody. The network people were lively, ambitious to a fault, and interesting, and the producers even more interesting, probably because they were writers, which made their profanity much more inventive and colorful.

While I was running the network relay, *The Cracker Factory* was finally published. I say "finally" because the prepublication process takes so long, you can forget you've written a book. "The book" seems like a dream you had long ago. Its arrival can come as a complete surprise.

When the first copy came to my house, my son Paul was so excited, he brought it straight to my office. With a smile like a sunburst, he thrust it under my nose. I stared at the cover. Oh my God, oh my God! It's real! It's here!

I jumped out of my chair and kept on jumping. Enthused, Paul joined me. Any network person going by in the hallway outside would have seen a thirty-something woman and an adolescent boy jumping up and down on an invisible trampoline. Undoubtedly they would have kept on walking, thinking that my office was being used for auditions. At the time, *The Donny and Marie Show* was on ABC, and they had some fairly weird acts.

Eventually we both calmed down. I asked Paul to take "the book" home with him. In my overwhelmed state, I felt that this copy of *The Cracker Factory* was the only copy in the world and I wanted it safe at home. When Paul left, I counted both blessings I'd been given: I'd held my own book in my own two hands and my son had been so happy for me, he'd dropped what he was doing and brought it to me. The first blessing thrilled me, the second touched my heart deeply and still does.

Just because I became adept at running back and forth with messages doesn't mean that I truly fit into network life. To be honest, I never thought of myself as a "network exec," but as a writer who'd fallen into network exec-ing much as Alice had fallen into Wonderland. I was there, round-eyed, breathless and clueless, on an excellent adventure. While there I learned to be a network exec because good people at the network and in production companies taught me, but I never got the hang of the politics. For one thing, I had no network ambitions. I had no desire to advance up the network ladder. I thought of myself as a temp who certainly would return to writing at some point, depending on when I got fired. I expected to get fired. Everybody with a job in television programming eventually gets fired. Those higher up the ladder get fired first.

Here's how it works. The Chief of Programming is in charge of Everything, the entire network universe. When the ratings are up and the network is number one, the sun shines on all, from Chief to cleaning crew. When the ratings begin to slip, and they always do because television is cyclical, everyone panics. At that point, no one knows what the network is doing wrong. Of course, when a network is Number One no one knows what they did right, either. This unrelenting unpredictability leads to network execs' high rate of mental instability, not to mention heavy drinking. At the point when the ratings begin slipping, all the panicked executives share one goal, "I <u>must</u> keep my job!"

With this goal in mind they look around for the problem/solution. The Chief points at the VPs of Drama and Comedy, "He/she is the problem! Fire him/her and all will be well." The VPs look one rung down the ladder at the Directors of Drama and Comedy, "He/she is the Problem. Fire him/her!" No one looks at the Program Executives because they (me) have absolutely no clout or impact on anything so they can neither be praised nor blamed.

Once all of the VPs and Directors have been fired (this cycle can take two seasons) the Corporate Headquarters guys (gray hair, gray skin, gray suits) look at the Chief of Programming, "He's the problem! Fire him!"

Once everyone is fired and a new group is hired, the next cycle begins. No one has figured out what went wrong because no one ever knew what went right, so the firing and hiring is the best they can do, given the lack of real knowledge.

In the immortal words of William Goldman in *Adventures in the Screenwriting Trade,* "Nobody knows anything."

Nobody that is, except William Goldman.

So my lack of personal identification with network life was easy, though sometimes it got me into trouble.

Every month, ABC's Chief of All Things Small Screen, Fred Silverman, flew in from New York Headquarters. Fred, the Great and Powerful, would gather the Meek and Lowly programming departments together in the conference room. There he would be presented with updates on current programming and also this season's pilot development. Development, because it was the future, always went first. They would discuss various pilot ideas and which ones might be successful. Fred would make some quick decisions or promise to greatly and powerfully think them over.

Then it would be the turn of the current programming department. We would present the story ideas given to us by each show's producers, or rather, wrested from them by threats of physical force. Producers always felt that their stories, like fine wine, should never be sampled before their time. Fred would then decide whether or not he liked the story ideas. Sometimes he'd make suggestions for improvement, a little nip here, a little tuck there. As a program executive the last thing you wanted to do was convey these "suggestions" back to the producers. They'd stare pop-eyed, then yell, "He wants one of the Three Wise Men to be a beautiful blonde! Are you *******crazy!" I always answered yes. Why not? It made them feel better and usually, they stopped yelling.

At one particular conference, a program executive in Current Drama was presenting upcoming story lines for the drama, *Family*.

Family of course was the very popular show starring Meredith Baxter, Kristy McNichols and as the matriarch of the clan, the Emmy winner Sada Thomson. As the executive read story after story, I began to giggle. They all revolved around Sada.

1. Sada tries to help Meredith with a project Meredith sees as her own. When the project goes south, Meredith blames Sada. Conflict ensues.

2. Sada does something and everything goes wrong.

3. + 4. Repeats of 2 but with more complications. I can't remember the specifics of 2, 3, and 4 but at that point I was beginning to notice that wherever Sada shows up, disaster follows. I do remember the specifics of the final two because who could forget them.

5. Sada goes to the bank and is taken hostage in a bank robbery.

(Oh Lord please don't let me laugh out loud. Oops, laughing.)

6. Sada visits a friend in the hospital and the patient in the next room jumps out the window.

"Don't let her come to my house!" I burst out, howling manically.

The program executive in charge of *Family* said through clenched teeth, "Please go away."

The other executives around the table expressed their agreement with vigorous nods of their heads and hand signs I translated as "shoo, shoo."

Fred, who by now was deeply enmeshed in his consideration of these stories, didn't notice. I left the room quietly, knowing I'd made a fool of myself and profoundly grateful to be out of there. I laughed all the way back to my office, shredding every particle of fledgling ambition that might be clinging to my uncomfortable and itchy power suit. I heard later that when the other execs told the story, they laughed, including the *Family* program exec, Brandon Tartikoff who later became a good friend. The difference between me and *real* executives was that *they* knew how not to laugh until it was safe to laugh.

At another network conference, the discussion turned to *Welcome Back Kotter,* another very popular show. The executive producer was Jimmy Komack who'd also created and produced *The Courtship of Eddie's Father*. Jimmy Komack knew how to present a successful show.

At networks, even the shows that are doing splendidly are looked at as one step away from failing. In television this attitude is called "keeping the heat on." In the real world it's called paranoia but the real world doesn't involve gambling millions on what is essentially guessing that a show will continue to be a hit.

In the interest of "heat" it was decided that the Kotters should have a baby. Babies and dogs are always good. A baby dog, a.k.a. a puppy, is best. One of my network executive buddies whose name I shall protect to the death, joked that the Kotters "should have quadruplets, one baby for each Sweathog" (you remember, Travolta was the hunky one). It was a joke. Everyone laughed. Except Fred. His eyes popped like golf balls.

"Eureka!" he said. "That's a fabulous idea! Go tell Jimmy Komack we want quadruplets. Imagine the publicity shots! Imagine the promos! Imagine the tune-in!"

At that moment my hapless friend was trying to imagine himself telling Emmy Award winning Jimmy Komack that his show was about to "jump the shark" (a TV term for doing an episode of a show wherein something happens that's so outrageous and incredible that it takes the audience straight out of the reality of that show to the eternal detriment of the show).

My friend's eyes were rolling around in his head and his face was beet red with panic when he suddenly realized that *he* wouldn't have to break the news. *I* would. He relaxed, shrugged and mouthed, "Sorry" in my general direction. I restrained my desire to kill him deader than dead.

I went to Jimmy and delivered the news. He stared at me. I stepped back, expecting spontaneous combustion. Instead, he just buried his head in his hands and wandered off mumbling, "Why me, God, why me?"

In episode twelve, the Kotters had quadruplets. In the next scene we saw the goofy but lovable Sweathogs each holding a baby (two sets of twins cast in a casting session that will go down in history – oceans of babies, all screaming). One by one the Sweathogs each handed a baby to either Marcia, who looked appropriately exhausted, or Gabe, who looked like he wanted to bite the infants. He hated the idea and said so, as did everyone else. Of <u>course</u> it was a *terrible* idea. It was meant to be **a joke!**

In subsequent episodes we never saw the quadruplets. They were always "sleeping." Once in a while we'd see Marcia holding a blob in a blanket, a plastic doll whose ill-timed shriek wouldn't wreck a joke. But mostly the quadruplets were "sleeping." The nightmare logistics of having one baby on a set were bad enough. The rules are firm and unbendable. To have a baby in a show you must have the infant's mother, a social worker and stand-in baby and the stand-in baby's mother and social worker. To have quadruplets in a show, you must have eight babies, four principle and four stand-ins plus all their "people" and accessories. Jimmy had good reason to ask God, "Why me?" The quadruplets "slept" through the run of the series. If the series was still on and the quads were thirty-two, trust me, they'd still be "sleeping."

While muddling through my accidental network career I was surprised to hear that ABC Television had bought the television rights to *The Cracker Factory*. Since my erstwhile agent was in Paree discovering that her swain was a less-than-noble man, no one had been working on this aspect of my book.

I found out much later (last Tuesday) that the actress Lana Wood had read the book, liked it, and brought it to her sister Natalie. Natalie read it, liked it, and wanted to play the lead role, Cassie Barrett.

Natalie wanted to option the book for her own company but ABC had beaten her to it. Out of courtesy, the executive in charge asked me to write the screenplay. As my screenplay progressed he requested changes, some so bizarre I thought that he must be sending me one-pagers from another movie of the week he was supervising. His requests had nothing to do with either my book or my life. His one-pagers tended to be single spaced seven-pagers, which also didn't expedite the process. Very often the suggestions he made on page one would cancel out the changes he made on page seven. Finally, after completing the script, he told me that he was bringing in another writer because "my script lacked drama." I told him that I was sorry my life was so boring, "I should have shot someone!"

In retrospect, he was right. At the time I'd never written a script and was trying to write one without knowing how. Again, I was writing an apple as I would have an orange. I wouldn't know the difference until I actually learned how to write scripts and wrote many of them.

A new screenwriter came in. Our first meeting at lunch took me aback.

"No one in this movie will smoke," he said.

"But Sir…begging your 'umble pardon…my book is about alcoholism," I bleated.

"I'm death on smoking," he responded, narrowing his eyes to make his point.

"Um…uh…the Cobb salad looks good."

What could I say? When you sell the rights to a book, the rest is out of your hands. The people who bought the rights take over. This is neither right nor wrong. This is business. If you write something and consider every word non-negotiable, then don't sell movie/film rights. The minute the writer cashes the check, the product is as gone as though it was a cracked pitcher he/she sold at a flea market. No one wants to buy a cracked pitcher at a flea market, then have a demented seller chase them down the street screaming, "Give that back, you cretin, it belonged to Aunt Tillie!"

When you're a writer, it's not easy to think of your material as a cracked pitcher but bottom line, that's what it is. The trick of selling material without serious seller's remorse is to sell to people who you know have taste. If the other kind, the crass and the careless, pop up first, wait. People with taste lurk everywhere seeking special material. You know who they are because they don't push their way to the front initially and theirs aren't the loudest voices.

The "special" person with taste and insight on this project

was Natalie Wood, who brought every bit of her immense talent and experience to this project. She played Cassie Barrett with a depth of feeling and such admirable restraint I could only stand back and admire. When I say that Natalie was good to me, I mean that she was kind beyond all expectations. In her relationship with me, there was not one "movie star" moment. She was what all of us would call a "real person," warm, thoughtful, and sweet behind the scenes.

She cared about *The Cracker Factory* as I know she did about all of her projects. Because she was Natalie Wood she had clout, so the people involved with the production had to listen to her suggestions. Because she had taste her suggestions were excellent and improved every aspect of the movie.

Because she cared about *The Cracker Factory*, she agreed to do extensive publicity for the movie. I appreciated that. Then she completely stunned me by insisting that I do publicity along with her. My first reaction was to run and hide in my closet.

I'd already done two book tours and had actually enjoyed them but only because I'd developed a strategy which had occurred to me on the set of *What's Happening?*

One of the actresses on that show played a character of extraordinary charm, sweetness, and humor. Offstage, this same actress was truly psychotic, angry, volatile, and given to carrying concealed weapons in her hair. Yet she'd come out on stage and beam at her public like Glenda the Good Witch and they'd go nuts applauding their love for her.

I used to wonder how she did that. So one night, standing in the wings, I was wondering how a writer who spends all her time hiding behind a typewriter in part so no one will know who she is, can suddenly sally forth on a book tour like a "public personality," a lecturer, a radio interviewee, a television performer, etc.

Then it struck me. I decided to pretend to myself that I was an actress playing a writer on a book tour. I did that until the stark terror of book tour appearances dissipated, though I must confess that the first time I wobbled onto *The Tonight Show*, I had to be pushed through the curtain by "crazy Shirley," Johnny Carson's able assistant.

But *this*, the movie publicity, my God...this was with Natalie Wood! I was terrified that I would embarrass her, so terrified that I knew that even my schizy but successful book tour stratagem would fail me.

Natalie took care of that. The first show we did was Merv Griffin. Natalie went on first. In those days "movie stars" didn't do daytime TV so Merv was thrilled to see her. While Natalie answered Merv's questions and gracefully steered the chat into *Cracker Factory* territory, she left me in the green room in the care of her husband Robert Wagner. R.J. Wagner then proceeded to tell me one funny story after another until I was called onto the set. I laughed. I howled. He was the funniest story teller I'd ever met and I knew dozens of comedy writers including George. By the time I actually walked onto the set and hugged Natalie, I was so relaxed from laughing I looked like a woman who'd been on TV forever. And so it went. Not only did Natalie include me, but R.J. went out of his way to make me feel comfortable. He's a class act as was she, all the way. I'm happy I had the good fortune to meet her. I cried the day I heard she was gone; I'll never forget her.

Thanks to Natalie and the *Cracker Factory* movie, my ABC career ended on a high note.

I had been thinking about writing a second book, about television, what else? Then someone offered me a job at Another Network. I opened my mouth to say no and instead, out of my big fat mouth floated, "Yes."

And so, again accidentally and again Alice-like, I descended to the Dark Side of Wonderland.

Chapter 13.

(INT. POLICE STATION)

This police station at night looks strangely cozy, like the place where Sheriff Andy monitored the whacky-but-lovable goings on in Mayberry. One side of the building is concrete and the other brick.

In television's olden days, Jack Webb, the most frugal of producers, shot many episodes of *Dragnet* here. To save time and money, he'd use the brick side of the building for one location, say "Exterior of Office Building in Encino," then have his crew drag the equipment around to the concrete side which would be "Exterior of Hospital, Los Angeles." *Dragnet* was a fixture at this station. All the officers loved Jack Webb who portrayed police officers as so upright that they couldn't bend at the waist.

Elena, flanked by Leslie and me, goes through the front doors. Dead ahead of us is the Security screening equipment. Behind it, a female police officer nods at the three of us.

Security Officer

Purses on the table, please.

We lay our purses on the conveyor belt then step through the archway. No buzzers are going off. No bells are ringing. No police dog is leaping at our jugulars.

Leslie

(to Security Officer)

Where is the missing persons department?

Security Officer

We're not the LAPD. We don't have departments. We have a squad room.

(points)

In there.

We follow the officer's finger. Leslie opens a door and we
go in.

Elena

I'm shaking. I'm nervous. I hate it here.

Leslie

We're with you, Honey. Don't worry.

In the squad room six desks are jammed so close together
that eavesdropping can't be avoided. Because it's night time only
two detectives are on duty, both wearing the de rigueur detective
uniform, dark pants and dress shirt with sleeves rolled up to the
elbows. We approach the tall thin one.

Leslie

We'd like to report a missing person,
Detective...?

He looks up at us, his eyes sighing. Paperwork, always paperwork.

Detective Elias
Elias.

He reaches for a form on a table behind him.

Detective Elias
(to Leslie)
Your name and the name of missing person?

Leslie
He's not my missing person.
(indicating Elena)
He's hers.

Detective Elias
(eyes sighing, to Elena)
Your name and name of missing person, please?

Elena
My name is Elena Perez. My husband is missing. He's Rick Perez.

Detective Elias
(to Elena)

When's the last time you saw him?

Leslie
(stepping in)
More than forty-eight hours ago.

Detective Elias
(to Elena)
Where was the last place you saw him?

Leslie
At their home.

Detective Elias
(deeply sighing eyes, to Elena)
Where was he going when he left your home?

Leslie
To his job at the Kasarian Box Company.

Detective Elias
(to Leslie)
Your friend can speak. I've heard her.

Leslie
I'm just trying to help.
(quickly)

As her friend, not her attorney.

Detective Elias

(suddenly alert, sharply, to Elena)

Why do you feel you needed to bring an attorney?

(accusing to Elena)

Were you and your husband having problems?

Oops! Now Elena and Leslie are both speaking at once. Detective Elias waits, seeming inclined to let them both rant for the moment. He knows that if he steps in too soon, they'll only get louder, not clearer. Knowing I can only add to the confusion, I drift over toward a chair near the second detective. I sit down in the chair. He looks over at me. The nameplate on his desk reads: Detective Shup. His hair is gray and he's built like a fireplug, squat and sturdy.

Detective Shup

Can I help you?

Cassie

No, thanks. I'm just waiting for my friends.

Detective Shup goes back to his paperwork. I watch from a distance as slowly, Leslie and Elena calm down. Whatever Detective Elias is saying seems to reassure both of them. They pull nearby folding chairs up to his desk. Now they're talking one at a time in low voices.

The door opens and a MAN comes in. He looks around, sees that the chair in front of Detective Shup's desk is unoccupied and approaches.

Man

The guy next door stole my chicken.

Detective Shup looks up. His expression doesn't change. His expression will *never* change. This is his game face.

Detective Shup

Your name please?

Robert

Robert Freeman. I live at 3854 Cumberland. My neighbor Jingo Blitz stole my chicken.

Detective Shup

You have proof that Mr. Blitz took your chicken?

Robert

My chicken is gone. Something in his bedroom is clucking.

(excited)

You got to come right away. He's going to kill my chicken!

Detective Shup

Are you aware that it's illegal to raise poultry within city limits?

Robert

(indignant)

Margo's not poultry! She's my pet. I can have a pet if I want!

Detective Shup

That's your inalienable right, Mr. Freeman.

(then)

Why would Mr. Blitz want to steal your chicken?

Robert

He's always complaining she makes too much noise. He says he can't sleep. He sleeps during the day.

(then)

He keeps yelling at me I should make soup out of Margo.

(then, upset)

Would you make soup out of your dog!

Detective Shup

There are statutes against that.

(then)

Mr. Blitz complains that he can't sleep during
the day, so he stole your chicken to kill her, is
that what you're saying?

Robert

Damn right.

(urgent)

You gotta send somebody right now!

Detective Shup

I'll have a black and white cruise by.

Detective Shup reaches for his phone.

Robert

(complaining bitterly)

Jingo's got no right to complain about noise,
not with people coming and going from his
house all night long. I'm the one not getting
sleep.

Detective Shup

(holding the phone)

What kind of people?

Robert

Those low lifes he sells to.

Detective Shup

Sells what, Mr. Freeman?

Robert

Used to be weed. Now it's that shit he
brews up in his kitchen.

Detective Shup

Uh-huh.

He presses a button on the phone.

Detective Shup

(into phone)

We got a meth lab on Cumberland.

Detective Shup gets up, reaches for his jacket.

Detective Shup

You stay right here, Mr. Freeman.

Robert

What about Margo?

Detective Shup

I'm sending a SWAT team to rescue her.

Detective Shup hurries out of the office. Robert looks
stunned.

Robert

(to Cassie)

You hear him? Ain't that somethin'?

(thoughtfully)

I gotta start paying taxes.

I notice that Elena and Leslie are heading for the door. Elena
looks very upset. I follow. I catch up with them outside in the
corridor. Leslie, who's stepped to the windows, is already on her
cell phone. Elena grabs my arm.

Elena

The policeman says I need to check hospitals.
He checked jails. Rick's not in jail.

Cassie

That's good.

Elena

I told him that Rick probably ran off with
some woman. He said I got to check hospitals
anyway. Rick's healthy as a horse. He can lift
one side of his truck straight up. Why would
Rick be in a hospital?

Elena looks worried. Leslie hurries over.

Leslie

A man fitting Rick's description was admitted to Good Samaritan. He got mugged in Silverlake.

Elena

We don't know anybody in Silverlake. Why would he....

    (angry again)

That woman!

    (furious)

No wonder he didn't call me!

Leslie

He didn't call because he doesn't know who he is.

    (to Cassie)

Amnesia. No ID. They want Elena to come right over.

Elena just glares at us.

Elena

I have to get home to the baby. I'll go to Good Samaritan tomorrow.

Leslie

But Elena...!

Elena

He doesn't know who he is tonight, he can wait. Tomorrow I'll go tell him he's a cheating pig.

Leslie

Wait. You're missing an opportunity, Elena. If he doesn't know who he is, he doesn't know anything.

(then)

When you see him, tell him he's a loving daddy and husband who worships and adores you. Take Lucy with you. He'll believe you.

Elena

Jesus Christ, what a whopper! How could you even think that up?

Leslie

(shrugs)

I'm a lawyer. Easy.

Cassie

We'll take you to Good Samaritan right now, if you'd like. You can call your neighbor and say you'll be late.

Elena

No, my neighbor gets up early for work.

Besides....

> (smiles at Leslie)

I got to memorize this story.

We leave the police station, heading for Leslie's car. None of us mentions the ethics of lying to a man who has amnesia. After all, how often is a woman who may have been betrayed offered the opportunity to turn a cheating pig into The Man of Her Dreams?

C H A P T E R   F O U R T E E N

NONE OF US LIKES TO THINK THAT WE ARE THE PRODUCTS of the times we live in or that we are influenced by them, but fortunately or unfortunately, depending on the times, we are.

I would love to believe that I sprang forth into the world unaffected by genetics or childhood environment, but I know better. I would love to believe that my attitudes, perceptions, and behaviors were not influenced by the times I grew up in, but that's not true. What's true of me is true for most of us. None of us lives in a vacuum.

I went to Network X in the Eighties when cocaine was the new drug of fashion for the LA rich and famous. Unlike ABC-TV where the ratings were high and the sun was shining, the ratings of Network X were circling the drain.

They'd recently hired a new and experienced Chief to rectify their downward spiral but even this tried and true ploy, bringing in the "Magic Man," didn't seem to help. Every time I entered the building, I walked through halls that smelled first of panic and then, as time went on, despair. No matter what Network X did, no one wanted to watch their shows. Cries of, "Damn them, what do they WANT!" echoed in the halls.

Deep down, everyone there knew that television is cyclical, that the audience will watch one network and/or type of programming for a while, and then inexplicably switch allegiance to another network or type of programming. We've seen this happen the last few years with the rise of reality shows. The audience loves them now and will continue to love them, until they love something else.

Everyone knew that these cycles happen as regularly as cycles of the moon, but people in television get paid a lot of money to believe that they can stop one cycle and begin another by sheer force of their brilliance and creativity. This is a delusion, but a powerful one.

I was at Network X for only a month when I realized I'd made a mistake. This was truly Wonderland: decisions made by the Mad Hatter, while caterpillars with hookahs sat around conference tables, acquiescing, "Yes, Master, and a very happy unbirthday to you!"

After a month of late night meetings that went nowhere but lasted until the wee hours, followed by very early morning meetings that went 'round, 'round, and 'round with no noticeable conclusion or decisions, I staggered into my office one morning, feeling like a complete failure.

Collapsing across my assistant's desk, I moaned, "I don't get it, Nancy. I'm the only person in this building who ever gets tired and hungry."

Nancy smiled her charming Deep South smile, "Don't you know, Darlin', they're all doin' cocaine!"

Oh my God! No, I didn't know. I was supposed to know, but I hadn't for a moment seen what was under my nose, or rather, going up their noses. By this time in my sobriety, I should have known a drug environment when I saw it, but in this case I was a rank "civilian" (what we in AA call you who are not).

I can only guess that an upbringing that emphasized that respect must be automatically granted to "authority figures," had left me partially oblivious to what should have been clear.

When I say "respect automatically granted to authority figures," I'm talking from the perspective of a female raised in a certain time and place, whose early childhood was controlled by a sternly patriarchal system of father, church, and parochial school. I tended to see "the guys in charge" as the guys in charge which I took to mean that they were also in charge of themselves. Alas, was I ever dumb!

Once Nancy pointed out the obvious, I began to trip over it everywhere I went. I saw big time producers bring gifts of coke to network executives hoping to curry favor. I participated in three-hour meetings where coked-up producers pitched ideas to coked-up executives. These ideas were discussed in excruciating detail, usually morphing into ever more bizarre ideas until, at the end, no one but me could remember the original idea which I never divulged because I usually fell asleep.

My image at this network wasn't good. When I discovered that the entire programming department went to a local watering hole after work one night a week, I inquired as to why I'd never been invited to what were obviously important networking events. I was told, "Because you don't drink."

I offered my usual cheery response, "Ginger ale is a drink." This time my cheery reply didn't fly. I was NEVER invited.

Even though cocaine use was viewed in that environment as lighthearted, hip, fashionable, and fun instead of serious drug use, for some reason these fashionable, fun people were clearly uncomfortable around straight-laced little me.

At Network X, I was so much and so obviously a fish out of water, that people were reluctant to cross my path. I'd taken on the aura of a black cat. I didn't fit in. A person who doesn't fit in, can be the bearer of bad luck.

Finally I put an end to the mutual misery. At a lavish Network X shindig, designed to celebrate the mythical future success of this sinking ship, I approached the only top executive who didn't flee when he saw me coming. I told him, "I hate it here."

His answer was sympathetic. "I know you do."

As soon as they could find my replacement, I was fired. Firing me was a nice thing to do because it meant they were required to pay off part of my contract. If I'd quit, they would have had no obligation. I didn't know that technical difference at that time, but the sympathetic executive, who couldn't ethically tell me himself, suggested that I call a certain entertainment lawyer who clued me in. I was very grateful.

After leaving Network X, I wrote a novel that was a fiction-alized account of that experience combined with a family story. The name of the novel was *Triplets*. After it was published, I heard from people I'd worked with whose reactions were surprising. Since I'd made merry fun of network life, I'd expected people to be irate. They weren't. Or maybe the people I heard from weren't irate, and the people I didn't hear from still want to kill me.

One network exec told me, "You remembered everything! And I thought you were sleeping through all those meetings!"

A co-worker I'd satirized, as I did everyone, went all over town bragging that he was the incredible jerk in the book, which would have astounded me if I didn't know that LA is a place where people don't care what you say so long as you're talking about *them*.

Merry network fun aside, the heart and soul of that book is the family story: the matriarch of the family tries to convince her adult triplets that they should help her move their father from his plain old grave to a new fancy mausoleum "because death is not the end of upward mobility." In that process, each of the triplets discovers that their memories and experiences of their individual childhoods is remarkably different.

I'd discovered this truism in long discussions with my twin brother and one-year-younger sister. As close as we were in age, the events of our childhood impacted each of us very differently. There were events that were pivotal to me that had either never registered in the memories of my brother and sister, or had faded immediately, and vice versa. I began asking other siblings I knew if this was true for them and discovered that it was not uncommon, so I had a theme I could write about. I loved writing *Triplets* and was thrilled to see it published.

During our childhood days, the "times" during which we

were raised and our parents before us had been raised, helped to form us. Our parents, most of them buffeted by the Depression and challenged by World War II, had hoped for, but not gotten, easier lives. They wanted us to have easier lives, but knew that life could turn on a dime. They knew disaster could come out of left field at any moment to crush and obliterate every person and thing they held dear. In the midst of post-war recovery and the baby boom, of Levittown and refrigerators rolling off the assembly line, our parents remained wary on a deep level. The "times" were upbeat, all surface smiles and the smell of new cars, but underneath, the subterranean vibe was the leftover jittery Forties reverb. Since little kids pick up the subterranean as quickly as they do the surface, we were a surfacely placid, but oddly jittery generation made no calmer just a few years later by the need to "duck and cover." Our parents had fought a war and won it. They'd given their all to make us safe. They gave it again, in Korea. Once again, we kids were safe thanks to our parents' generation. Unfortunately, we couldn't feel safe and didn't because we had a big fat Bomb hanging over our heads. It never went off, but we were told every day that it could. It just hung there over our childhoods, a terrifying piñata at everyone's birthday party. Our war, like our collective childhood, was cold and serious like the grave. This wasn't anyone's fault. It was "the times we lived in."

Again, at Network X, I saw an up close and personal example of how "the times" can affect us.

So many of the "fun, hip, and fashionable" people I knew had their lives ruined by "dabbling" in cocaine. They didn't take the drug seriously at the time. Only later, when talented people in the entertainment community were burning out, dying, getting fired never to be hired again, was the drug seen for what it was. The people who wouldn't take the drug seriously at the beginning, were having too much fun. The blinders they put on were intentional. They didn't want to see where they were going and what they were doing to themselves. Cocaine was the ticket to the best parties and back stage passes.

The power of drugs and alcohol is that they obliterate our innate understanding that consequences will ensue. With substance abuse, there's no tomorrow. There's only today and what feels good RIGHT NOW. But acknowledged or not, the consequences roll in and wash us away.

When I talk about "the times," I also mean that when substance abuse becomes an accepted part of any culture, many more people "dabble" than would have otherwise taken the risk. That means that many more people get hooked. And many more hooked people die or end up wandering aimlessly, no longer themselves, but addicts in search of their drug, now their only priority.

One of the nicest, kindest, most good-hearted people I've ever known got caught up in the Eighties hip, fashionable fun, just dabbling to be sociable you understand. He didn't want to be thought an outsider. The last time I saw him he was sitting on the sidewalk in front of a liquor store at 8 AM, a pint of low rent booze in his hand. He appeared to be nodding off. He didn't recognize me when I said hello. He and his good heart were gone. At that moment at least, he was unreachable.

I went home and sat there, trying to think about nothing, until the pain of the loss of this nice person became bearable. It still hurts my heart.

Chapter 15.

(INT. MEETING ROOM)

Welcome again to our Tuesday Night Women's Group. Pull up a chair, but shhhh. Elena is telling her story.

I'm as interested as everyone else, but I glance at my watch, wondering why Leslie is late. Since she's very much a part of Elena's story and even, in some respects, the hero, I expected her to show up. Leslie's personal life may be confusing to her but her lawyerly skills are FORMIDABLE and she enjoys pointing that out.

Elena's all wound up and talking fast.

Elena

The hospital was a nightmare. It took them over an hour to find Rick.

(shakes her head)

You'd think that they had patients with amnesia tucked in every nook and cranny.

(then)

It's a rare condition, right? Maybe one in a million. So they have ONE guy in the place who doesn't know who he is and they didn't know where they put him! Is this dumb and dumber or what?

Katherine

(becoming impatient)

But you found him.

Elena

(nodding, yes)

No thanks to them!

(then)

The head nurse told me that they don't have a psych ward so they put Rick down on the surgical floor. He's in a room with a guy named Eddie who had his gallbladder taken out. All this Eddie guy does all day is swear and fart, but that's guys for you, isn't it?

Katherine

(whispering, to Cassie)

She's getting a mouth on her, isn't she?

Elena

I heard that, Katherine.

(shrugs)

I know what you're thinking. I used to be so sweet. Well....

(then)

Once I found out that Rick was cheating, I decided that sweet is for women whose guys don't chase tramps.

(smiles slowly)

But that don't mean I won't be sweet again.

Elena laughs and we laugh with her, though we're not certain why. Maybe we're just happy to see her laughing.

Elena

So the nurse takes me in to see Rick. She tells him that he has a visitor. I lean over him. He looks up at me. I see this blank expression.

> (grinning)

I say, "Hello. You are Rick Perez. I am your wife, Elena."

> (then)

His eyes start rolling around like a pinball machine. "You can't be my wife!" he sez.

"Why not?" I ask, ready to clobber him.

> (smiles)

"Because," he sez, "you are so beeeyoutiful!"

Everyone

> (automatically, sincerely)

Awwww.

Elena

> (nodding)

That's what *I* said.

> (then)

So I told him about Lucy, and his job at the

box factory, and who his friends are, and
where we go to church, and everything else I
could think to tell him.

Rachel

What happens now?

Elena

The doctor says that his head scan is okay. No
big concussion or anything. I can take him
home tomorrow.

Terri

And then what?

Elena

He eats, he sleeps, he watches ESPN. He goes
back to work. We have sex on Friday night
after the news.

Terri shakes her head, no. That's not what she meant.

Terri

I meant, will his memory ever come back?

Elena

The doctor doesn't know.

Rachel

He cheated on you. Why are you taking him back?

Elena

Rick doesn't know that.

(then)

Here's the plan. When Rick comes home, I'll treat him like a king. He doesn't remember my drinking. Not a minute of it. He's forgotten everything I put him through. Least I can do is forget his cheating. Clean slate both ways.

Rachel

And if he remembers later?

Elena

I'll make sure that life is so good he won't want to mess it up, no matter what he remembers.

(then)

It's a second chance for both of us. Who doesn't want that?

(then)

Is that wrong?

Rachel

(to Elena)

God knows I'd give anything for a clean slate.

Your H.P. is giving you the green light for The
Big Do-over. Grab it!

(whispers to Cassie)

First thing when I get home tonight, I'm
hitting Stan over the head with a hammer.

Katherine

I love happy endings. My turn.

Cassie

Katherine?

Katherine

Last Saturday I went to the Senior Center. I
heard from a neighbor that they have bus
trips to the wine country.

(off curious looks)

Not that I'm going to drink wine! Lord, no.
That's the last thing I'd do! Can you imagine
an old lady wino? I met one once...on a
twelfth step call. Pathetic. All covered with
bruises from falling down. Frail as a sparrow,
too. My sponsor Gloria and I didn't know
what to do. She was three sheets and dehy-
drated. We called an ambulance. I think they
put her in some kind of home.

(shudders)

God forbid. God forbid. God forbid.

(then)

Anyway, I hear that the wine country scenery

is pretty so I thought, why not? Do me good
to get out and see something new. They even
give you a box lunch for four dollars extra.

   (then)

So I'm talking to the sign-up lady and she's
telling me what a nice trip it is. She says that
it ends at a winery with samples they give you
in the tasting room. So I'm telling her that I
won't be drinking any samples, thank you
very much and she asks me why not. So I tell
her about AA and this group, and the poor
thing starts crying. She tells me she wishes
she could get her husband to stop his
drinking, but he can't or he won't. And the
only place he'll go where there isn't any booze
is the Senior Center where he likes to play
cards.

   (deep breath, excited)

So, I told her that our group will find some
AA men. We'll bring them to the Center to
start an AA group for both men and women.
Two weeks from Thursday. We're all volunteered.

   Katherine sits back, takes another deep breath and closes
her eyes, waiting.

Rachel

You volunteered ALL of us!

Katherine

   (pleased with herself)

Yup.

Rachel

But I have Stan and the kids and…work
and…jeez!

Terri

I don't know what to say to old people.

Katherine

You have no trouble talking to me.

Terri

That's YOU! You're Katherine!

Katherine

They have names, too.

Terri

Old people don't like teenagers.

Katherine

Are you nuts? Their grandkids are teenagers.
They'd give the rest of their teeth for a five-
minute phone call from a grandkid.

(smiles)

They'll love you.

Terri thinks about that.

Terri

I never had grandparents.

Cassie

All that's needed to start an AA meeting is two drunks and a coffee pot. I'll go to the Center. Katherine will go and I'm sure we can find a couple of guys from the men's group. I'll ask at the open meeting tomorrow night, too. We'll have plenty of volunteers.

(to Katherine)

Did you ask the Center if they want us to come?

Katherine

What Senior Center wouldn't want an AA meeting?

Cassie

(laughing)

This is one of the reasons we love you, Katherine.

(then)

I'll call the Center tomorrow. If they want us, we'll go. If they don't, you can bring your new friend some Al-Anon literature. There're Al-Anon meetings in this hall on Saturdays at noon.

Katherine

I'll bring her myself.

> (smiles)

At least she'll learn how to live her own life.
No sense in letting some drunken old goat
rule her roost and run her show.

Cassie

You're the best, Katherine. Terri?

Terri smiles shyly, a girl with a secret she's about to spill. She looks around to make sure she has everyone's attention.

Terri

I got a job, a real job!

Everyone

Hey, congrats! That's great! Where? Doing what?

Terri

I'm a bag lady.

> (off puzzled looks)

I bag groceries. At Ralph's. The big one on San Fernando Boulevard.

> (then)

I went in and applied and got the job! Yaay for me!

(enthused)

I figure I can work my way up to cashier.

After that, who knows?

(then)

The people there seem real friendly. I talked to one of the cashiers. She's been there eight years, her name is Margie. She says she started there when she was a little older than me, right after high school. She said that everybody gets along and the customers aren't bad either, except when management changes the aisles around and people can't find the toilet paper. Then she hears all kinds of complaints but she doesn't blame them. She said that management mostly has their heads up their asses with their surveys and polls but they're decent people to work for so she has no complaints.

(then)

I think I might like it there. It's better than part time at the dry cleaners and there aren't any toxic fumes that I know of.

Cassie

We're proud of you, Terri.

Everyone

Yeah, Yes, we are.

Elena

When do you start?

Terri

Friday morning. I could work evenings which
I would like because I'm a night person but
then I would miss this meeting.

(hesitates, then finally admitting)

I like this meeting. I didn't before but now I
do. My friend Lynnie told me I'm lucky to
have this group. She said I've changed. I don't
act like I have barbed wire up my…behind…
any more. Well, not all the time, anyway.
Lynnie thinks that's a good thing.

(finishes quickly)

So, I'm working mornings so I can be here at
night.

Cassie

That's great Terri. The group wouldn't be the
same without you.

Katherine

You HAVE changed Terri. You're not texting
during the meetings anymore.

(benevolently)

That's real progress.

Terri

Thank you, Katherine.

Rachel

And you're much, much cleaner.

Terri

That's random, but thanks.

Rachel

(leaning close to Terri)

You're going to make something of yourself, girl. I have a hunch. Stay clean and sober and you'll have a future.

Terri

Thanks, Rachel. One day at a time.

I lean back in my chair, watching Terri bask in the approval she's earned. In AA, real progress is rewarded with real approval and one gets to bask. For most of us, our last basking moment before AA was long in the past, so both the approval and the basking take some getting used to. Taken together, approval for our real efforts combined with the ability to accept it, feels a lot like the jackpot — serenity.

I'm glancing at my watch again. Where is Leslie? I'll call her during coffee break.

Christa

Hey, hey, I'm back! Give me a hand, you gorgeous creatures!

Rachel, Elena, and I get up and run to greet Christa, our traveling member, who's toting a big cardboard box. Gone for weeks, our Christa is dressed like Seventies hippie or '09 Bohemian, whichever reference you can relate to. Her green and rose swirling skirt contrasts brilliantly with her long curly red hair.

Rachel

Hey! Hi! Welcome back! Give me that box!

Cassie

You were supposed to be back three weeks ago! Where have you been?

Rachel and I take the box from Christa's arms. It isn't heavy, only unwieldy. We take the box to the table and place it in front of Katherine so she can see the contents when it's opened.

Christa

You know me. When I'm on the Road, I've got to stop and smell *all the roses!*

Elena

How do you feel?

Christa

Got an alligator? I'll wrestle the bastard.

Rachel

(obviously concerned)

You sure?

Christa places her hand on her heart. Her eyes roll dramatically.

Christa

Scout's honor, mama.

>   (noticing Terri)

Hi, Sweetie, you new? I'm Christa.

Christa holds out her hand. Terri, who's obviously become shy in the face of Christa's flamboyant personality, shakes Christa's hand.

Terri

I'm Terri. I'm a little bit new.

Christa

Welcome, welcome.

>   (grins at Katherine)

You're looking foxy, Kathy.

Katherine

>   (grinning back)

And you look like the Queen of the Gypsies.

>   (then)

Thanks for the postcards you sent me.

>   (explaining to everyone)

Black and white pictures of trash dumps with lipstick hearts all over them.

>   (then, kidding)

Who takes pictures of trash dumps?

Christa

Avant-garde artists, like me.

>   (to Elena)

I can't believe how big Lucy is! Can I hold her later?

Cassie

>   (afterthought)

Oh. Coffee break.

Katherine

>   (laughing)

That horse left the barn two minutes ago.

Nobody goes to get coffee. We stay at the table with Christa, who taps the box with one long gold-shimmer fingernail.

Christa

>   (re: the box)

I brought you presents from the world's longest flea market sale. Guess what they are?

Katherine

Fleas?

Christa

Too obvious, Katherine. Shame on you.

Rachel

Needlepoint pillows with obscene sayings.

Christa

(sounding disappointed)

Sorry, I looked but I couldn't find any. People must be passing their obscene pillows down to their next generation.

Cassie

Old political campaign buttons? If you have an old "I Like Ike," I'll take it. He looked like my grandpa.

Katherine

IKE looked like everyone's grandpa, 'till he made a speech. Then he sounded like everyone's grandma. Natter, natter.

Christa

You know I hate politics. It's all mumbo-jumbo and the man behind the curtain. Guess again.

Rachel

(tired of guessing)

Bullet proof vests. Karaoke machines. A meth lab in a box. Widgets.

Christa

> (laughing)

Okay, okay. I'll tell.

> (ta-da dramatic)

Salt and pepper shakers!

We applaud enthusiastically. Who doesn't love old salt and pepper shakers? Besides men, of course, and people who don't understand that the ever-evolving American style can be seen in the history of salt and pepper shakers.

Christa

> (re: the box)

I made a grab bag. I rolled each pair up in bubble wrap. Just reach in and grab one. If you don't like yours, you can trade. I won't be offended.

We reach into the box. I pull out a plump bubble wrap cylinder. I pull at the tape then unroll the cylinder. In a second, I'm looking at two faux Hummels, a boy and a girl with little holes in their heads. Which is salt and which is pepper, I haven't a clue.

Since I'm a twin with a brother, I should be loving these shakers. Truth is, I'm not a big fan of Hummels, faux or real. Those figures with their round blank eyes, too wide smiles and painted cheeks remind me of Howdy Doody, who gave me nightmares. I thought that Buffalo Bob was probably a nice guy but Howdy Doody? Save me, Mommy!

I look around. Katherine has unwrapped her shakers, two large ceramic cubes colored the most beautiful, watery sea glass blue-green – I must have them!

I'm wondering if Katherine will trade me for the Hummels when Terri unwraps her shakers, two cartoon-like, big-eyed, black and white penguins.

Terri
(squeals)

Wow! Terrific. I love them!

Thank you.

Christa

I got those in Pennsylvania.

Katherine
(re: her cubes)

I had shakers like this years ago in the Fifties. But they still look very modern.

Christa

I got those in West Virginia.

Terri gazes up at Christa, clearly on the verge of hero worship.

Terri
(shyly)

I love your hair.

Christa pulls off her wig. She's bald as an egg.

Christa

I got this in LA.

Terri jumps a foot. None of the rest of us do.

Christa

(to Terri)

Christ, I didn't mean to scare you, Sweetie.

Rachel jumps up to stand beside Christa. She seems really angry. She shakes Christa's shoulder.

Rachel

(accusing)

You had a relapse! You didn't call us!

Katherine and I look on. We'd already guessed.

Christa

I was busy having chemo at Sloan Kettering.

(then)

Great hospital. Great people. They let me send out for sushi.

Rachel

(still angry)

You should have called us.

Christa

To do what? Worry?

   (then, hugging Rachel)

You know I hate to talk when I'm feeling crappy.

Rachel

Yeah, but still....

Rachel hugs Christa back.

Terri is still staring at Christa, who notices Terri's stare.

Christa

   (to Terri)

It's okay, Sweetie, I'm fine. Everything's under control. I'm going to be around for a long time.

   (smiles)

I even made some new AA friends in New York.

   (then)

None better than you guys, of course.

Cassie

You've been back for a while, haven't you, Christa?

Christa

   (reluctantly admitting)

I needed a little time to get myself together.

Christa pops her wig back on her head and adjusts it.

Christa

I got the same style in blonde but I think red is sexier.

 (then)

Is this a coffee break or what?

 (pointing at Cassie)

We better have real milk.

Cassie

We have real milk.

 (to Terri, nodding at Christa)

She's bossy, she's picky, but we let her stay. We are *such* nice people.

Rachel, Elena, and Terri follow Christa to the coffee area. I take my faux Hummels and slide over next to Katherine. I show Katherine the figures. I point at her cubes.

Cassie

Swap?

Katherine's eyes widen as she sees the Hummels. She snatches them out of my hand.

Katherine

Done.

I take the cubes from the table and put them in my purse.

Cassie

    (to Katherine)

Two lumps and a chocolate chip cookie?

Katherine

Two lumps and *three* chocolate chip cookies.

I head for the coffee area. I'm halfway there when I remember that I'm worried about something. I stop. What is it? Hell of a thing when you forget what you've been obsessing about. They should invent a pill to help you remember what it is you're obsessing about to go along with the pill you take to make you stop obsessing. That would be a best-selling two-fer that Big Pharma could take to the same bank where they take the rest of our money.

Got it!

I'm worried about Leslie. I pull out my cell, catching a glimpse of my cubes. Ahhhh. They are the color of an old soul, drifting in for its final incarnation.

I dial Leslie's number. Her line rings and rings. Her voice mail doesn't pick up.

I have a hunch. A dark hunch. I find Rachel at the coffee urn.

Cassie

    (to Rachel, quietly)

You've got to come with me right now!

C H A P T E R   S I X T E E N

I KNOW HOW TO KILL YOU AND GET AWAY WITH IT. I KNOW how to dispose of your body. I know how to construct an airtight alibi for my whereabouts at the time and place of your untimely demise. I know how to frame someone else for your murder. I know what to say to the cops when they interview me, so they thank me for my help instead of arresting me.

I come by these enviable skills courtesy of Executive Producers Joel Steiger and Dean Hargrove, who taught me how to write mysteries.

They hired me to be the Story Editor on the mystery series *Matlock* even though I'd never worked on a series or written a mystery. This hiring in itself would be a mystery if it hadn't been, like everything else, an unplanned event in a series of events in an accidental life.

In retrospect, landing on *Matlock* was the nearly logical outcome of having done a series of television Movies-of–the-Week, a career path that chose me while I was making other plans.

After I left Network X and wrote my novel about network life, *Triplets*, I was once again, in the strange space known as "Prepublication." Like The Late Great Catholic Limbo, once dogma, now defunct, Prepublication is the place where you wait.

When I was a kid in Catholic school, we offered many a

mandatory Mass up to the Almighty for the sake of the Souls in Limbo. This soul population, so we were taught, was primarily composed of babies who had died before they could be baptized and other innocent but unbaptized souls. According to the Sisters in charge of teaching us what to believe, the souls in Limbo were happy but bereft. Though Limbo was taught as a place of joy and delight, not unlike Disneyland with free food but without waiting lines, these unbaptized souls would never see God up close and personal. Of course, I wanted to go to Limbo, primarily because the God I envisioned was a lot like my father, unpredictable and given to intemperate rage. What kid in his right mind would want to sit close to that? I wanted to spend eternity in Limbo, the happiest place in the Catholic quad: Heaven, Hell, Purgatory and Limbo. But alas, I'd been baptized so Limbo was off-limits to me, even before the Church caused Limbo to mysteriously vanish. An edict came from the Vatican and Limbo was no more, gone like the pterodactyls. The Sisters most likely tried to explain this in terms that kids could understand, but failing miserably, had to fall back on their all-purpose "because the Pope says so, that's why."

Prepublication Limbo is different. It's all waiting without the fringe benefits. When I finished and delivered a book, my usual practice was to spend a couple of weeks staring into space. My head would gradually adjust to living in one world instead of two, "book life" and "real life." As "real life" re-emerged I'd notice everything I'd neglected while traveling in "book life." Where did all this dust come from? Who threw my sweaters in the washing machine – they're all shrunken and shriveled! Oh right, that was me. Where did all these take-out menus come from? Apparently we've been eating only pizza and kosher Chinese. Where did I put George? Did we always have that black and white cat?

Once I tidied up and found George, I'd resume exercising. Up and down steps, round and round blocks, determined to return to a healthy lifestyle, whatever that was. That was me in Prepublication Limbo, happy to be schlumping along peacefully, going to daytime meetings again, seeing more of my family and cooking from the latest copy of *Cooking Light*.

This Limbo was different. It was interrupted by an out-of-the-blue phone call from Peter Stern, a former colleague at ABC television who was now an executive at CBS Television. Peter was at ABC at the time when *The Cracker Factory* was published and later filmed and had liked both the book and the movie. Now CBS was about to do a movie with a similar theme. Peter asked me, in his gentlemanly way, if I would be interested in writing a TV movie about Adult Children of Alcoholics. Would I??

Writing this movie of the week, *Under the Influence*, was the best experience I've ever had in writing for television. Not only was I able to write about a subject that was important to me, but Peter Stern and his fellow CBS executives were helpful and supportive beyond any writer's expectations. They treated me as though I actually knew what I was doing and would do the very best I could.

The movie had a great cast: Andy Griffith, Paul Provenza, Season Hubley, Dana Anderson, Joyce Van Patten, and in his first ever movie role, Keanu Reeves, as a kid with a serious drinking problem.

The director was Thomas Carter and the producer Vanessa Green, a spirited, funny and talented woman with a sharp eye for human psychology. Thomas was a young and brilliant director who'd come from the series *The White Shadow* with Ken Howard. Vanessa wondered if he would feel comfortable working with a woman producer and writer. She asked me if I played basketball. I told her that basketball was my favorite sport and that in high school at Our Lady of Girls Can't Jump, I hadn't done badly according to our coach, an eighty-two-year-old nun.

Vanessa arranged lunch at her house, which had a basketball hoop hung over the garage. Thomas arrived, all good humor and excellent manners, prepared to meet with "the ladies." Ten minutes later we were all shooting hoops in the driveway, yelling and having a really good time. Forty minutes later we were friends, ready to dig into Vanessa's lunch and the project that was a high point in my life.

I loved and admired Thomas Carter and Vanessa Green. I

loved their energy, their talent, and their enthusiasm for the movie. Naïve as I was at the time, I thought that most directors and producers, even those lacking their talent, possessed their positive and professional attitudes. I would find out how wrong I was later, but at the time, my ignorance was bliss.

I'd seen one of his great movies, *A Face In The Crowd*, at least ten times, so I was an Andy Griffith fan. In *Under the Influence*, Andy played the alcoholic father of a family who'd become dysfunctional because of his drinking. This role was the polar opposite of "Sheriff Andy" and he dug deep to play it. Outside of *A Face in the Crowd*, this is still my favorite Andy Griffith role because of the nuance he brought to it. I've never seen another actor whose face can simultaneously project a wide charming smile and the glittering, dangerous eyes of a snake. Incredible.

The new guy in town, Keanu Reeves, would pour his heart and soul into every take, then ask Thomas Carter if he could do it again. He was so nervous about his performance, which was pitch perfect and very moving, that on the night of the screening at the Director's Guild, he wouldn't go into the theatre. He paced back and forth on the sidewalk outside until Vanessa went out and begged him to come in, telling him that he was among friends. But he wouldn't or couldn't. I understood how he felt. It was my first movie, too, and in my heart, I would have preferred pacing outside on the sidewalk with Keanu than actually sitting through the movie.

My kids came to the screening. Paul, Jack, Ellen, George and I made up half a row, sitting behind Vanessa and Thomas.

My kids didn't have to come to the screening. I left it up to them. They came to support me. I knew at the time what a brave thing that was and appreciated it more than they knew. I could only imagine how it must feel to be the teen/adult kids of an alcoholic mother watching a movie about teen/adult kids in an alcoholic family. Though I'd told them that the kids in the film weren't based on them, but on research I'd done, I'm sure they wondered. When the movie was over, they told me they liked it. I was so relieved that I didn't actually care what anyone else thought.

That movie did well in the ratings, so of course I was approached to do other movies of the week.

The first offer was an adaptation of a romance novel that had been optioned by an actress who had fallen in love with the book. This actress, known for her plastic surgery and equally plastic performances seemed to think that this novel had movie potential because the heroine, an incredibly wealthy woman, wore incredibly beautiful clothes. The fact that it had no story, incredible or otherwise, left her undaunted. She planned to design the wardrobe herself and so turn this opportunity into a two-fer, a movie and the launch of her designing career. I thought that perhaps I could improve the story, so I met with the star. She was pleasant but adamant. She "adored" the book. She didn't want the story improved. What she wanted was black and white Art Deco sets that would showcase her wardrobe designs. She wanted on-set perfume diffusers wafting Chanel #5 to "set an elegant atmosphere." She wanted a much younger leading man, one who could perform the magical trick of making her look younger while he himself appeared mature. She wanted me to infuse her character with the wit and charm of Coco Chanel even though the character in the book she loved had all the wit and charm of a clothes hanger. She wanted and wanted and wanted. I only wanted to get out of there.

I did many drafts of that movie before I gave up. Other writers succeeded me. The movie was never made. I assume that no one could solve the problem of how to change the story without changing the story. That, as they say, is show biz.

Because I had written *Under the Influence*, which was viewed as a "social theme" movie, I was asked to write a movie about a woman whose teenaged son repeatedly beats her up. I was a third of the way through writing the story when I realized that I had no understanding of a mother who would allow her son to beat her up. None. A fellow writer advised me to "make it up." I didn't know how. The concept was so foreign to me and the mother's various responses so unnatural that I couldn't write six acts of this woman trying to cope before she finally calls the cops and gets herself and the kid some help. To put it bluntly, this idea bummed me out. I quit. This movie was never made either, probably because it bummed everyone else out, too.

Which taught me a lesson. Most of the ideas hatched in network meetings and agents' brains should never see the light of day. It's not that they're flawed. Everything human is flawed. But some ideas are so abominable, they should be drowned at birth and never spoken of again, not even in whispers. Remember *Supertrain*, the NBC drama debacle that lasted ten minutes? It cost NBC so much money to make that they couldn't buy another new show for almost six months. That train never should have left the station.

One of the problems inherent in writing TV movies is that you seldom know the people who hire you until you actually start working with them. I contracted to write a movie for a real rascal, a producer who sold his idea to NBC by promising he could deliver twelve popular country western artists as the stars. The truth was that this producer couldn't deliver a pizza, never mind a star. To make matters worse, he wanted a story with equal parts comedy, mystery, romance and music. When he said equal he meant it. When I delivered the first draft, he read it, marking each line as C for comedy, D for drama, M for mystery and MC for Music to Come. This time it took only one draft for me to realize that this man was coked out of his mind. I fled and didn't look back. He never paid me for my work and disappeared to Spain "for his health." I believed that. Apparently he owed some shady, short-tempered people a lot of money.

A movie script I loved writing was called *Dr. Elsie*, based on the life of Elsie Giorgi, MD, a wonderful woman and physician who played a big part in the founding of the Watts Clinic.

At my first meeting with Dr. Giorgi, I was so impressed with her life and her personality, that I immediately asked her if she would be my doctor. When she agreed to take me on as a patient in her busy practice, I was very grateful. Her practice was varied, ranging from the people she saw at the Watt's Clinic to Hollywood's celebrity A-list. Everyone loved her for her down-to-earth manner, her skill as a doctor, and her amazing intuitive diagnostic gifts.

She made each patient feel like the only patient in the world. If you went to Elsie with a cold in the morning she would call you in the evening to ask if you felt better.

Her life story would have made ten fascinating movies. The part of it I told was her lifelong relationship with her soul mate, a Mafioso who spent some years in jail only to die within a short time after his release. There was also a mystery in the movie but I didn't care much about that. What I wanted to capture and doubt that I did, was the love in her eyes when she spoke about him.

I finished the script in record time, partly because it was a pleasure to write and partly because the Writer's Guild of America of which I was a member, was about to call a strike. I delivered the script to Joel Steiger and Dean Hargrove and went home to wait. It turned out to be a very long wait. The Guild called the strike the next day. The strike dragged on without good results for a long six months during which my picketing assignment turned ironic. With my fellow writers, I carried my sign up and down the sidewalk in front of Network X, where occasionally my former colleagues would wave at me from the windows. I'd wave back, wiggling my sign over my head and envying them their air conditioning. After years as a member of the Writer's Guild, I've noticed they strike and picket only during the weeks in Los Angeles when the daily temperatures exceed one hundred degrees.

When the strike was finally over, I got a call from Steiger and Hargrove that unfortunately, the *Dr. Elsie* project had dead-ended. After six months on strike, the project seemed like old news and was scrapped along with most all writers' scripts, now also old news, that had been in development at various networks.

But they added, almost as an afterthought, that since they'd liked my script and since Andy Griffith who starred in *Matlock* had liked my script for *Under the Influence* and since their Story Editor had just left the show, would I like to come over and work on *Matlock*?

I hesitated, then decided to be honest. I told them I didn't know how to write mysteries. They told me that they already knew that because they'd had to jam the mystery element into *Dr. Elsie* themselves, mapping out the mystery steps while I lost myself in the love story. Their story "suggestions" had been so nicely expressed, I hadn't noticed that they were actually great chunks of story they'd dropped into my head.

I learned that series television is a collaborative venture. People sit in a room together and make up a story. When the story is done, one of the people goes off alone to write a script. Then everyone gets together and discusses the script. Then the script gets rewritten. Then it gets cast and then it gets filmed. If that sounds like clockwork, it's because it is. In series television, there's always a deadline. Come hell AND high water, every seven working days, the cameras are going to roll and there had better be actors in front of them with a new scripted story to tell.

I love deadlines. They focus my mind. They keep me in my chair long enough to get the work done. Deadlines keep me on track. They provide a finish line, a clear definition between work and play. For this reason, I loved writing for series television with its endless demanding deadlines, culminating in that golden moment when I could type "The End" on the current script.

A story editor's job is more rewriting than writing. In the course of participating in twenty-two story meetings and rewriting twenty-two scripts that first season, I learned how to write mysteries.

From the same office and for the same people, I also wrote for the series *Father Dowling Mysteries*, starring Tom Bosley, Tracy Nelson, Mary Wickes and James Stephens, *Perry Mason* starring Raymond Burr and eventually, *Diagnosis Murder*, staring Dick Van Dyke who's every bit as nice as I thought he would be.

These shows, often referred to as "bloodless" mysteries were designed as family fare, the kind of mysteries the audience could watch without cringing. No twisted criminal minds here, no gruesome carnage, no psychosexual pathology or expository psychobabble. Just a dead body on the floor with all its parts intact and little if any blood, waiting for the eventual arrival of the lawyer, priest, or doctor who would solve the crime.

"Whodunnit" was the question, and that answer, hopefully entertaining, would arrive in exactly forty-seven minutes and forty-six seconds with commercials and network promos to round out the hour.

My favorite among them was *Father Dowling Mysteries* because the cast, besides being wonderful actors, were all good human beings. I never heard a cross word from or about Tom Bosley. Though he will always be "Mr C" to me, he wore Father Dowling's collar with warmth and good humor, providing me with an opportunity to write about a parish priest I'd always wanted to see in my own parish pulpit.

When Tracy Nelson began filming the show, she was wearing a wig – and not a flattering one either, more like a dead squirrel plopped on her head. The wig was necessary because Tracy was still undergoing chemotherapy for Hodgkin's disease. She never missed a moment of work, never lost her spirit or extraordinary kindness and never complained. Throughout the most difficult time possible, Tracy's perseverance could only be described as gallant. She knew that I was a big fan of her father's music and generously shared with me stories about Rick Nelson, whom she adored and missed terribly. I knew without a doubt that her father would have been as proud of her character as of her acting. I know that I admired both, more than I can say.

Mary Wickes was a hoot, an old-fashioned word for a lady who was up-to-date until the moment she passed away. Stories? Mary had hundreds of stories, going back to a play she'd done with the legendary Lunt and Fontanne. While I was supposed to be in my office like a good little writer typing my heart out, I'd be on the set listening to Mary tell stories and laughing until my sides ached. I wouldn't have traded the times I played hooky to listen to Mary for any "power" lunch with any studio mogul. She was absolutely unique. There won't be another Mary Wickes, ever. I'm very fortunate to have known her.

Another actress I admired for her talent and tenacity was Mariska Hargitay. Though she came in often to read for parts, she was never cast for any role in any of the mysteries I worked on. I couldn't understand why. No matter what role she was reading for, her audition was always the best. She was always prepared, always intelligent and always brought considerably more to the character than was written on the page. I didn't have the last say in casting or even the first, so I would sit back and watch her performance, then wander back to my office mystified when she didn't get the role. I would have given up but she didn't. Mariska Hargitay was a woman undaunted by the vagaries of her profession. When she won her well-deserved Emmy for her fine work on *Law and Order: Special Victims Unit*, I jumped up and cheered.

Writing is work that's done in solitary, whether it's a calendar for the PTA newsletter or a script for a high-budget Bruckheimer TV show. In the former, the PTA news-mom sits in a room alone sweating over every word, dash, and dot. In the latter, a script writer sits alone in a room, sweating over every word, dash, and dot. The difference is that outside the script writer's room, real live television stars are waiting to read the words, dashes, and dots. That's the only difference. All writers who write, try to do their best. All writers who write, give their work their best shot. Of course, the script writer's rewards are larger but a larger award in the marketplace is no indicator of the value of the writing. Those magazines they hide behind the counter make tons of money. The Cancer Survivor Newsletter makes none. The Cancer Survivor Newsletter has better stories, and you don't have to take a shower after you read them. Reward has little to do with value.

I'd like to give all the writers of PTA newsletters, flyers for charitable fundraisers, and any document sent from a teacher to a parent to praise his/her child a writer's award, preferably cash and lots of it. To quote President John F. Kennedy, "Life isn't fair." That goes for the lives of writers, too, the sung and unsung.

While I was writing one mystery after another, life, as it does, went on happening. My son Paul and daughter Ellen went to college. My son Jack married a lovely, warm, and funny girl named Cyndee. Paul and Ellen graduated. Ellen came back to Los Angeles to begin a career. Jack and Cyndee had their first daughter, Becky, making me a grandma at thirty-eight. Paul became a teacher and married his forever sweetheart, a wonderful girl named Teryl who is both my daughter-in-law and dear friend. Ellen married a man who George and I loved instantly, Mark Saraceni, whom we would have adopted if Ellen hadn't said "yes."

My kids as adults are strong and compassionate people. I'd like to take credit but I know better. Even George, their dad and rock solid anchor, doesn't take bows for what they grew into. Our kids set their own goals and made their own decisions. They chose their own paths and continue to walk them with a humor and grace that leaves me humble. Where did these terrific adults come from, these complex and honorable people who call me Mom? They overcame an early childhood with an alcoholic mother, the toughest of situations for any kid, and there's not a self-proclaimed "victim" among them. They're my kids and I love them, but even more, I like and respect them.

A lot happened while I was writing mysteries, all the truly important stuff in life, all the fun stuff and sad stuff and proud stuff and goofy stuff – all of these moments I tried to capture in photos. Since I wrote mysteries for ten years, I have boxes and boxes of photos.

Every morning during those years I would wake with the knowledge that everyone I loved and everything I had was mine, only because I'd stayed sober. Without the sobriety I'd found in AA, I would have died early and drunk. There would have been no boxes of photos and certainly no photos of me at the weddings of my sons and daughter.

During those years and after, up to the present, I wouldn't have been alive to see Jack and Cyndee's kids, Becky, Katie, Emily and Hank – Paul and Teryl's kids, Rendle and Kayla – Ellen and Mark's kids, Carl and Joe – or to give them the big gooshy kisses all grandmas love to give.

I would never have seen the arrival of granddaughter Katie's son Jackie and granddaughter Becky's son Owen and his baby brothers and sister: the triplets Quinn, Liam and Isla Rose.

AA didn't just save my life. It gave me the rest of my life to live.

Chapter 17.

"Why are you so worried about Leslie?" Rachel asks, as I turn left onto Glenoaks Boulevard heading for Glendale. "Everybody misses a meeting once in a while."

"This is different," I tell her.

"No it isn't," Rachel insists. "To tell you the truth, I didn't think she'd stick around. She's so nuts about that married boyfriend of hers, she doesn't think about anything else. It's not like she's working her program."

"I know she isn't."

"Well, that's up to her, isn't it? If she doesn't want to get sober, she won't. You can't make her. You know that. You DO know that, don't you, after all these years?" Rachel sighs, "You won't catch me chasing meeting no-shows in thirty years."

"I don't chase no-shows," I said. "If the people who come to AA want to go out and try drinking again, that's their business, not mine. I can't make anyone do anything. I just hope that eventually, they'll come back. But Rachel, this isn't about drinking."

"You just lost me."

"I have a hunch. I hope I'm wrong, but I have a bad feeling."

"About what?"

"About Leslie, what else?"

Rachel looks at me curiously. "You get hunches?"

"Drinking isn't the only Irish curse," I say enigmatically and speed up just a little, to squeak through the changing traffic light.

Leslie's apartment building is one of those California court-yard complexes immortalized in *Melrose Place*. Leslie's complex is upscale and well maintained with lighting and a courtyard garden complete with benches and a fountain.

I knock on Leslie's apartment door, calling her name. "Leslie, it's Cassie and Rachel. Open the door." I knock again, more of a banging this time.

There's no answer.

"She's out," Rachel decides, turning to go. I reach for my cell phone, then dial 911. Rachel looks nervous. "Who are you calling?"

When the operator comes on, I tell her that I'm at the address of a suicidal friend who isn't answering her door.

"Can you send someone, or should I smash a window and get in that way?" I wait for the answer knowing what it will be. "Thank you. I'm at 1249 Benefit Avenue, apartment 201, ground floor. I'll wait for them here."

I click off, then turn to Rachel who's staring at me with dropped jaw. "The police will be here in a minute."

"Leslie's going to be madder than hell. She's probably out drinking and you're having the cops break into her house!" Rachel's eyes got bigger. "And what if she's in there with the boyfriend and just isn't answering?! Holy shit, she'll kill you! And the cops are going to arrest you for filing a false alarm!"

I hand Rachel my car keys. "Sorry, Rachel. I wasn't thinking. I shouldn't have dragged you along. Take my car and go home. I'll call a cab."

"Are you bleeping nuts! I'm staying. Somebody has to go over to your house and tell your husband you've been hauled off to the pokey. Jeez girl, please, please don't ever have a hunch about me!"

I see a police car pulling up. I move toward the two officers who are slowly, slowly emerging from the car. "Officers?"

The officers ask my name and address, then ask me why I think my friend is suicidal.

"She told me she's going to kill herself," I lie, while Rachel stands beside me, appalled and blinking furiously. If I'm right about Leslie, I'll tell Rachel that Leslie was threatening suicide in every way except words. Actually, I hope I'm wrong, but who can take the chance when it comes to a life?

The officers open the door and go in. Rachel and I follow. Rachel mumbles to me, "The last thing I want to see is naked Leslie and naked boyfriend screaming at us. I'll go wait outside."

Rachel retreats to the doorway. I follow the officers.

We find Leslie in her bathtub, her wrists cut and an empty bottle of Jameson's on the tile floor.

An officer checks the pulse in her neck. "She's alive."

The second officer calls for an ambulance.

Later, outside, Rachel and I watch as paramedics slide Leslie's gurney into the back of the ambulance.

"We're going to follow the ambulance to the hospital?" Rachel asks. It's a rhetorical question. She assumes that we will.

"No. Leslie's safe. Time to go home. Our husbands will be worried," I remind her. "We'll see Leslie in the morning."

"But when she wakes up in the hospital and they tell her she almost died…well, I'd freak out, wouldn't you?" Rachel is clearly worried. "Shouldn't we be with her?"

"We will be, tomorrow. Leslie needs some time to think about this before we all run to her rescue," I say, thinking about my first morning in the psych ward. I woke up in a strange room not quite knowing where I was or remembering how I got there. Left alone with myself in those early hours, I came to my own understanding that I was in very deep trouble. Leslie needed the same kind of time to come to her own conclusions. If she was lucky.

"Okay," Rachel agrees reluctantly, then asks, "Do you have hunches about anything else?"

"Yeah, if I don't get some sleep, I'll be crabby as hell." I smile at Rachel. "Time to go home."

*   *   *

St. Joseph's Medical Center has grown from our local hospital to one of those medical centers that specializes in EVERY-THING and is equipped with machines that do everything but hold your hand while you pass away. For that, we still need loved ones, brave, caring loved ones whose prayers at our bedside carry us on wings to the unknown other side.

I find Leslie's room. She's sitting straight up against her pillows staring at her bandaged wrists. She's looking shocked and confused as though she's wondering who might have attacked her. I know that look. I've seen it in alcoholics over the years and in the mirror when I was drinking. She doesn't remember a thing. Leslie did what she did in an alcoholic blackout.

As I enter the room she looks up. "Cassie!" She bursts into tears.

I don't try to stop her from crying. I know that tears are good for her. I hear what her sobs say. There's guilt, remorse, shame and profound anger, all directed at herself. The defenses she's worked hard to maintain, the wall against her own feelings, are crumbling. This is good.

Suddenly Leslie shakes her head violently to stop her own crying.

Too soon, I think. Not good.

"That's enough of that," Leslie announces. "I have to pull myself together."

"Why?" I ask. "Do you have an appointment?"

Leslie looks at me, shocked. "No. I just have to…you know…pull myself together." She runs the fingers of her bandaged hands through her hair. "I called the office a half hour ago and told them I sprained my ankle and I'll be in tomorrow." She gives me a wry smile. "How dumb is that? Now I'll have to limp around the office for a week. I wasn't thinking it through."

"It's hard to think things through when you're drunk and hung over," I tell her.

Leslie glances my way but doesn't make eye contact. She speaks very quickly. "If the partners at my office knew what happened, that would be the end of my career."

"They can't fire you for a mental health issue. It's against the law," I remind her.

Leslie winces at my "mental health" reference but moves past it, fast. "They're too smart to fire me outright. They'd welcome me back with phony smiles, and then let me rot in my office. No case assignments, no clients, no meetings, nothing. Eventually I'd quit, end of problem." Leslie finally makes eye contact. She gives me a winning smile. "You know how it is with the boys' club. If it was one of them, they'd stand up, no matter what, even if the guy murdered his family. You know how that works, don't you?"

"The boys' club isn't your problem," I say, not returning her smile.

Leslie looks at her wrists, again in wonder. "I'm not sure how this happened."

"It didn't HAPPEN, Leslie. You did it." I pull up a chair. "Why?"

For a moment it seems that Leslie will cry. Instead she swallows hard, twice. "David dumped me," She says, in the voice of a sad little four-year-old. "He came over to my apartment last night. He said that he'll always care about me, but…" Leslie covers her face with her hands. It's several seconds before she continues, "But he can't continue to cheat on his wife. He said she's not well and he…"

I see the tears trickling through her fingers. I hear the sorrow of loss in her voice.

"And you believe him?" I ask.

The fingers fly from her face. Her wet cheeks glisten. Her eyes spark. "Of course I believe him! Why wouldn't I believe him? His wife isn't well and he…" Now Leslie's crying.

"If his wife isn't well and he gave a damn about her, he wouldn't have cheated on her in the first place. You know that, Leslie. Just like you know that David is just one of those guys who cheats on his wife until the latest girlfriend wants more. Then he drags out his line about the sick wife and backs out the door. Deep down you know it. You know you've been had."

"No, I haven't!" Leslie shouts at me. "David wouldn't do that to me!"

"But he did, Leslie. You know he did. And you know that you're not the only woman he's hurt this way. Not the first, not the last."

"Are you trying to make me feel worse?" Leslie demands.

"I'm trying to make amends to you, Leslie. I've sat in meetings and listened to you lie to yourself and never gave you honest feedback. I was waiting for you to come 'round in your own good time. You never asked for advice. I never gave you any because you and I are a lot alike. When people gave me unsolicited advice, I used to think they were telling me what to do. So, I'd do the opposite. It took me a lot of years to realize that the people who gave me advice, good or bad, cared about me. So I'm making amends. I'm sorry. I haven't been a good friend."

Leslie stares at the ceiling not knowing what to say.

"Do you remember cutting your wrists, Leslie?"

"No." She says this in a very small voice.

"Do you remember deciding to drink?"

"Vaguely. Not really."

"Did you have the bourbon in the house or did you have to go out and get it?"

"I had it in the house," Leslie admits, then adds quickly, "for David, not for me. He likes a drink once in a while but he doesn't have a problem."

"That's why we call him Mr. Wonderful," I say.

"That's nasty," Leslie shoots back.

"I certainly hope so," I tell her. "Are you scheduled to have a psychiatric consultation?"

"Yes, but I'm going to skip it. I feel a lot better. This won't happen again." Leslie bites her lower lip. "They can't keep me here if I sign myself out."

I take Leslie's hand. "I'm here because I care about you. Everyone in the Women's Group cares about you. We'll all be here tonight for a meeting. We'll bring coffee and cookies."

Leslie looks confused. "But I might not be here tonight."

"You want to go home and call David and tell him what happened so he'll know that you love him so much, you almost died for him. You think he'll come running over to say he's made a terrible mistake and he wants to be with you forever."

Leslie gasps. She's speechless.

"You aren't the first Leslie and David I've known. Only the names change, Honey. No matter how unique you feel, this is a very old story." I squeeze her hand. "You'll be here tonight and here's why. If you go home today without the help you need, you'll drink and you'll die."

Leslie turns away but I see the tears in her eyes.

"David isn't your problem. Alcohol is your problem." I hold onto her hand. Leslie tries to pull away. "When David dumped you, you reached for a bottle, instead of a phone to call us. Any one of us would have come right away, to take you to the meeting. But you didn't do that. The only decision you made last night was to reach for that bottle. After your first drink, alcohol made all the decisions. You drank a whole fifth. You could have had alcohol poisoning. You cut your wrists. You were drunk so you didn't cut deep but you could have. Or you could have gotten into your car and killed innocent people and yourself. If you had a gun in your house, you could have blown your brains out. You would have been dead without wanting to be dead because once you took that first drink, your ability to choose was over. Over. Just like your life."

Now Leslie is crying hard, but her hand has relaxed and she leaves it in mine.

"When the psychiatrist comes in, tell him or her that you have a drinking problem with underlying issues. Say you need help. ASK for help. LISTEN to what he or she says. Be sure to say that you're a member of an AA group, so the psychiatrist knows you have some support."

"I'm not exactly a walking AA endorsement." Leslie sounds bitter.

"You never exactly got on board either." I'm blunt. "After this you might decide you want to start working your program. Or not. It's up to you." I withdraw my hand. "I've got to go. Think it over, Leslie. You're not alone. We're here for you. You can make it." I kiss her cheek. Leslie doesn't pull away. "We'll be back at six-thirty. All of us."

* * *

It's six-thirty and we're back, even Katherine leaning heavily on her walker. We pause outside Leslie's door.

"I don't know what to say." Terri's nervous. "I've never even thought about killing myself."

"Good for you, honey," Katherine says. "You're like me. We'd rather kill other people than kill ourselves."

Terri looks alarmed. "I don't want to kill anybody!"

"That's because you're a sweetie pie." Katherine beams at Terri. "But I'm old and cranky. I have a list."

Rachel glares at Katherine. "Stop that right now. You're

frightening the child. She takes you seriously."

Katherine glares back. "You should, too. You might be on the list."

"Please stop," Elena begs. "How are we going to help Leslie if we're all squabbling?"

"We're all squabbling because we're worried about Leslie," I tell them. "We're all afraid that if we say the wrong thing, she'll jump out the window."

"How did you know?!" Katherine demands, looking surprised.

"Because I'm worried, too," I confess. "I'm not a shrink. I don't want to make Leslie worse."

"Leslie's still here," Rachel points out. "She didn't check herself out like she told you she might. So whatever you said to her didn't make her worse."

Katherine shrugs. "Maybe they put her in restraints so she couldn't leave." We all stare at Katherine who shrugs again. "Since when did Leslie ever listen to anybody?"

"Are we going to go in?" Terri asks. "Or are we going to stand here in the hallway all night? I can't inhale much more of this Lysol. It makes my eyes water."

"We'll go in," I decide. "This will be our regular Tuesday Night Women's meeting only it's Wednesday. We're not here to do therapy."

"We need to remember that Leslie's had a relapse, so she's basically a newcomer," Rachel reminds us.

Terri nods. "This is like, her first meeting."

"Back to step one," Katherine agrees. "She's powerless over alcohol and her life is unmanageable."

Terri grins. "That shouldn't be hard. I mean, look where she is!"

"I've known people dying of cirrhosis who still claim they

don't have a drinking problem," I say. "Denial is a lot stronger than logic. It's the Crazy Glue of addiction. You can't pry it loose. We have to want to give it up."

"What if Leslie doesn't?" Katherine asks. "What if she throws us out of the room?"

"What if a meteor crashes through the ceiling? What if San Francisco attacks Los Angeles? I can't answer 'what ifs'," I say, sighing. "The worst that can happen is we go to the cafeteria, have a heart healthy snack and go home. Okay?"

"The cafeteria has pecan rolls as big as your head," Katherine remarks. "When I was here for my hip replacement, a nurse brought me one every night."

"There you go." I smile at Katherine. "Whatever happens, we eat."

I lead the way into Leslie's room.

"Hi, Leslie," everyone says at once. Our group hello is accompanied by group cheery smiles. Leslie smiles back. Her smile is different from her usual tight grimace. One would call it almost serene. "Hi, Ladies. I hope you brought me a meeting."

"Jeez, you seem almost normal," Rachel expresses our group surprise. "I mean, better than usual. For you."

"We did bring a meeting," Terri tells her. "I'm glad you want one."

"Are you ready to listen?" Katherine asks, sounding like everyone's mother. At this moment, I'd like to poke her but I'm afraid she'd fall over.

Leslie doesn't seem to mind. "Yes, yes and yes," Leslie says. "But before we begin the meeting, I want to tell you that I'm going to rehab."

"You're kidding!" I'm shocked.

"No, I'm not," Leslie says. "I talked to a shrink who sounds like he's known me all my life. Christ, that guy has me down to my last nut and bolt. I could swear he's been reading my diary except I don't keep a diary. Anyway, he laid it all out for me, the rest of my life if I keep doing what I'm doing. It isn't pretty, believe me. In fact, he scared the living hell out of me. And he was right. If I don't do something about it now, I'll end up a bag lady mumbling in the street. I could see it in front of me, like a movie. The shrink said I should forget about my job and my...personal relationship...for a while and shoot my ass into rehab. So, I'm going." Leslie smiles. "I picked Hazleton because it's got a great reputation. I need somebody to drive me to the airport tomorrow at two."

"You got it," I tell her.

"She listened to a shrink and not to us," Katherine whispers to me, sounding miffed.

"Who cares?" I whisper back. "Leslie's going to rehab. That's all that matters."

We begin the meeting. While I take care of group business and we read from the Book, Terri scoots down to the cafeteria to get us those pecan rolls as big as our heads.

C H A P T E R   E I G H T E E N

For the children of alcoholics

I WON'T PRETEND TO KNOW WHAT IT'S LIKE TO GROW UP in the scattered care of an alcoholic parent or parents. My parents weren't alcoholics.

My children know what it was like and so does my husband, George. Both of his parents were alcoholics at a time when no one knew anything about the disease. George grew up during the Great Depression when life was bitterly hard even in families where parents didn't drink. He not only survived, but took care of his younger brother, Carl. He made sure that Carl got to school on time and in clean clothes. He insisted that Carl go to Mass with him every Sunday because he saw the church as a rock they could cling to in the turbulence of their lives. His mother died when he was eleven and Carl was ten. The cause listed on the death certificate was gall bladder disease but he and Carl both knew it was alcoholism. His mother, a frail and pretty woman, was only thirty-one when she died unexpectedly. The school principal called George and Carl to his office to tell them that their mother was dead.

When they were in high school, the attack on Pearl Harbor changed everyone's lives. George and Carl both joined the service the second they were old enough. George picked the Marines and Carl joined the Army. Their father, Jack Burditt, also joined the service, choosing the Navy. On one memorable occasion they all met on liberty in Hawaii and went out together, a Soldier, a Sailor and a Marine. George told me that they talked about the war and the future, not the past. Never the past. In those days no one talked about alcoholism, least of all the kids who'd grown up with it.

My own kids can talk about alcoholism. They have and they do, to the people they choose. Who they talk to and what they say is none of my business. They have a life experience I've never had. There are people who understand that experience far better than I do.

There's only one thing I can say to you children of alcoholic parents, whether you are six or sixty, one thing I know for certain, this is the truth: your parent's drinking was/is not your fault. It was NEVER your fault. You didn't cause your parent to drink. There's nothing you could have done to stop your parent from drinking. Nothing. If you had never been born, your parent would still be an alcoholic.

Your parent may have told or be telling you that you're driving him/her crazy, that if it wasn't for you...blah, blah, blah. That's a lie. When we parents are drinking, we lie. We say horrible things to our kids and every word is a lie. Drinking makes liars of even the nicest people, who are anything but nice when they're drinking. You MUST NOT believe a word your parent says when he/she is drinking. Not a word, not even the maudlin apologies we make so you'll like us again. Don't listen to us. We lie.

Please get help. From a sober relative, a teacher, or a friend. Your parent's alcoholism isn't a secret you need to keep. It isn't a secret or a shame for you to hide. You deserve all the help you can get. Tell somebody you trust and ask for help. Keep asking until you get it. A happier life waits for you, I promise.

If you're an adult, you still need help and deserve to get it. You deserve to have the therapy you need to unravel your past. You deserve to find peace wherever and however you can. You are suffering from alcoholism just as much as your drinking parent. You don't need to feel like a victim for the rest of your life. There's help waiting for you, whether in a Twelve Step program or the private, or group, therapy of your choosing. You didn't ask for this. You deserve better. You can cut the past loose with help. Thousands have done it. You can, too.

For the spouses of alcoholics

I can't imagine what you've gone through. My spouse isn't an alcoholic. I can't imagine your feelings as you've lived with a person whose drinking has impacted every day of your life. I can't imagine the burdens you've shouldered alone that were meant to be carried by two in a marriage. I can't imagine how lonely you've been through it all.

I can only say, again, that none of this is your fault. None. Your spouse drinks because he/she is an alcoholic. You can't fix what you didn't break. You didn't make this person an alcoholic. You can't sober him/her up, no matter how much you want to. You can't argue anyone sober, or reason anyone sober or pray anyone sober. We alcoholics not only lie, we don't listen. If we get sober it's because we've had a moment of clarity, discovered that our problem is alcohol and made a decision to do something about it. No one but the alcoholic can do that. All the love and caring in the world won't sober anyone up. That's tragic and heartbreaking for both alcoholic and spouse, but it's also the nature of the disease. We alcoholics don't get sober until something "clicks." Spouses can't make that "click" happen. No one can.

If your alcoholic is abusive, you need to leave him/her. The apology that follows abuse is another lie, this one meant to manipulate you into staying. Once an alcoholic becomes abusive, he/she STAYS abusive, until hopefully sobriety arrives and the alcoholic goes into intensive therapy for the underlying issue of anger management. If you stay with an abusive alcoholic, waiting and hoping, chances are you will die or be severely injured. That's hard to hear and harder to act on, but it's true. Without drinking spouses, the battered women's shelters would be nearly empty.

Spouses can go to Al-Anon which, like all AA based groups, is free. At Al-Anon the family members of alcoholics share their experiences, strengths, and hopes, just as we alcoholics do at AA meetings. No member of Al-Anon ever feels ashamed or alone because they learn from other members that shame is unnecessary and inappropriate and that they are among friends who will support them no matter what.

If you feel that Al-Anon isn't for you, then find the help you deserve through a therapist or a group. Usually your local hospital can help you find what's available in your area and of course, the internet is a great source. There are online Al-Anon meetings also, but I do recommend face-to-face meetings because all of us in an alcoholic household tend to be far too isolated.

Please get help. Your life is as important as the life of the alcoholic you've made the center of your thoughts and concerns. *YOUR LIFE IS IMPORTANT. YOU ARE IMPORTANT. IF YOU LOOK IN THE MIRROR, YOU WILL SEE THE MOST IMPORTANT PERSON IN YOUR LIFE.* Maybe you don't feel that way now, but with help you will. You'll know that the only life you can change is your own. You'll know that you deserve a better life than the one you've been living.

From my heart, I wish you well, children and spouses. I wish I could make everything better. I can't. But you can. Hard as it is, please try.

To those who relapse

You've been to detox or rehab or AA or some other program and still...every day is a battle you sometimes lose. You've read books about alcoholism, researched your disease online, talked to your doctor, your friends, and your family, but still...when the bottle beckons, you think "one can't hurt."

Your rehab, friends, family, program have given you sound advice and all the tools you'll ever need to grasp and maintain sobriety, but still...nothing plays as loud in your head as the conviction that "one can't hurt."

You want those around you to understand how hard you've tried. You want your therapist, your group, your employer, your spouse, your kids, your boyfriend/girlfriend, your pastor, your case worker to understand that this battle is hard and you do your best every day in your struggle against this incurable disease. If you've isolated yourself, you want the self you see in the mirror to understand and grant you absolution.

It's not going to happen. You don't get a free pass. You've gone to a program and learned about your disease. You know what to do. Stop making excuses and do it. Do it today and don't stop doing it until your white-knuckle abstinence turns into sobriety. It will. But only if you stop telling yourself the lie that "one won't hurt."

"One won't hurt" will kill you.

"One won't hurt" will put you behind the wheel of a car driving erratically toward a family of four who doesn't deserve to die at the hands of a self-pitying addict who was taught what to do and didn't do it.

"One won't hurt" will unleash all the anger that lies beneath your depression and turn it into violence toward your child.

"One won't hurt" will whisper to you that the only way out is suicide, the sooner the better.

"One won't hurt" will allow you the satisfaction of telling off your boss, your spouse, the police officer who pulls you over, the whole damn world that doesn't understand, that you're the helpless victim of an incurable disease.

You *NEED* the "one that won't hurt" because you have so much stress in your life.

Here's the *NEWSBREAK,* "helpless victim": *EVERYONE* has stress in their lives. Everyone. There are no exceptions.

I've known people in AA who stay sober despite lost jobs, foreclosure, chronically sick kids, broken marriages, family deaths and their own terminal illness. They stay sober because they've continued to reach out for the help they need and deserve. They stay sober because they've learned to work their programs. They've stayed sober because they have enough problems without adding a relapse to the list. They stay sober because living sober with help is easier and better than living drunk, high, and crazy. They've stayed sober because they've made their sobriety their number one priority for so long that it's become second nature. Sobriety is the "pearl of great price" we read about in the Bible. We will go to any lengths to keep it.

If the program/therapy/approach you're using now isn't working for you, find another one. No one claims that AA or any other method works one hundred percent for everyone. I don't claim that. AA works for me but if it doesn't work for you, it's your obligation to find the method that does. Like the diabetic whose life depends on a drastic change in lifestyle, the responsibility is yours and yours alone.

If sobriety isn't your number one priority and you don't suffer from a mental health issue, stop whining about how hard it is to maintain sobriety. You can do it. Many, many, many of us have and so can you. Stop choosing "one can't hurt" and your life will get better.

Life is hard. Life isn't fair. We're all human. These are truths.

All of us have these truths in common. Not one of us, from the wealthiest media mogul to the guy eating soup at the Midnight Mission, escapes the personal grief that is part of life. True, the wealthy and connected bang their heads against the walls of mansions instead of hovels, and recover from their strokes in high-end rehab instead of an overcrowded hallway at County General, but none of us gets through life without trouble.

Given that truism, we're all in this together. We're here to receive help when we need it and give it to others the moment we can. Simple as that.

If you've been living the life of "one won't hurt," it's time to stop. Maintaining sobriety isn't a board game, two steps forward and one step back. It's a terminal illness, a loaded gun. Stop playing with a disease that will kill you. The next "one won't hurt" is the step off the cliff.

You hear what I'm saying? Stay sober or die.

You think I'm being mean. Yes, I am. I'm being bitchy mean because I care. In my forty-one years of sobriety, I've attended far too many funerals for people who thought that "one can't hurt."

To alcoholics and addicts

I've been where you are. I know how hopeless, confused and tormented you feel.

I also know that there's help available to you.

If you've heard of AA but you're not sure what it's about or if it might work for you, there's a simple way to find out. Look up Alcoholics Anonymous in the phone book. There will be a listing for "Central Office." Call that number and ask where you can find an "open" meeting. An "open meeting" is a meeting for both men and women. The person will give you the locations and times for several meetings in your area.

Go to a meeting. Sit in the back. No one will ask your name. Someone may say "hi" but no one will intrude on you. There is no membership list. There are no dues or fees. AA is free and open to everyone.

Once you're sitting in the back of the meeting, try to listen. Notice that the people around you are sober. When you hear something that you can identify with, and you will, don't panic. Nobody has been reading your diary. We alcoholics all tend to feel, act, and react in similar ways. Just continue to listen.

You can leave at any time. There's no hall monitor. Everyone at the meeting is there in pursuit of their own sobriety. No one will try to stop you if you want to go.

But come back. Listen again. You can do this over and over for as long as you want. Maybe you'll decide that AA can help you. If you do, AA will. Simple as that.

If AA isn't for you, then please find help somewhere else.

As I've said elsewhere in this book, I'm a believer in thirty-day (or longer) medical rehab which includes AA meetings and then AA meetings for follow up.

Significantly, *ALL* rehab programs, even those that cost fifty-thousand dollars, recommend or use AA as aftercare along with whatever other services they provide. These medically-based programs view AA as an effective partner in recovery.

The combination of rehab (or psych ward back then) and AA worked so well for me, I have to admit to a bias. Evidently, independent research supports my bias so I feel comfortable in strongly recommending both in combination.

The thirty days gives you a chance to get clean and sober, get sound medical advice, gain some clear-headed perspective and begin finding your way. Your doctor or local hospital can help you get into a rehab program. Taking the thirty days is the least selfish thing you'll ever do in your life. It's not running away. It's standing up to the problem that's wrecking your life.

I wish I had a spray can of "Booze Begone." I'd spray it in gallons from crop-dusting planes. No one would have a problem. But I don't have a spray can or a magic wand either. Neither do you.

What you have is an illness that has no cure, but like diabetes, can be arrested and maintained.

You know that you have to stop drinking "someday." "Someday" is right here and now. No matter what you might think at this moment, the words "sober" and "happy" *CAN* go in the same sentence. I know that you're scared. I was scared, too – scared out of my mind. I'm not saying that seeking sobriety is easy. I'm saying it's worth it. And it gets easier, much, much easier until the cravings are gone and the new sober life you've built is yours to keep.

Reach out. Find the many hands reaching out to help you. The hands belong to your doctor, therapist, minister, rabbi, priest, local AA group, rehab program in your area, hospital…there are many hands for you to grasp and hold onto.

You're not alone. You deserve all the help you can get. Please take that first step, that small leap of faith, and I promise, help will be there for you as it was for me.

Chapter 19.

Welcome back to the Tuesday Night Women's Group.

We're taking an early coffee break. Since the first half of our meeting has been all about Leslie instead of sharing, I thought maybe we could get the topic out of our systems if we took a break.

Our "Leslie talk" isn't exactly gossip. We're worried about her. Will she stay sober? Won't she? Was Hazleton the right choice? Of course, Hazleton is always the right choice, but what is Leslie's motive? Is she intent on getting sober in one of the best facilities in the country or is getting the hell out of Dodge and away from her problems her primary motivation? Is Leslie trying what AA calls, the "geographical cure" which is the term for an alcoholic who suffers from the delusion that by moving to a new location, one can leave "the problem" behind? Since "the problem" is the alcoholic himself/herself, hauling one's alcoholic self from Pittsburg to Los Angeles isn't a "cure," but an opportunity to drink oneself to death in a better climate surrounded by palm trees.

So, our "Leslie discussion" is continuing over Rachel's coffee and a plate of bear claws from Martinez Bakery, a gooey treat brought by Katherine and Terri who decided that our group needs "cheer-up" food. Once Leslie was safely off to Hazleton, a thoughtful gloom settled over the group. The "Leslie discussion" took a turn for the guilty.

Katherine

She could have died. Every time I think about it, I get the shivers.

Rachel

We didn't help her enough. We didn't say the right thing.

Katherine

We said too much about her boyfriend.

Elena

No, we didn't say enough. We all thought he would dump her because that's what men like him do, but we didn't tell her.

Cassie

Would she have believed us?

Terri

If you guys told me that my boyfriend was a jerk, I'd stop coming to meetings. I'd tell you to get your nose out of my business.

    (hesitating, then scared)

I didn't know you could be in AA and still want to kill yourself.

Cassie

There's a difference between warming a seat

and taking the program seriously, Terri.

(then)

Coffee break's over.

(suddenly remembering)

Almost forgot, Christa went to Med Spa. She'll be back with us next week.

(then)

Elena?

Elena

(smiles)

As you all know, Rick still has amnesia. And you know that I've fed him a pack of lies about how lovey-dovey we are.

(then)

Well, it's working. I act lovey-dovey to him, he acts lovey-dovey to me. Thank you St. Theresa, we're the loviest, doviest people I know!

Katherine

But it's a lie!

Elena

(adamant)

How is it a lie? I act like a good wife. He acts like a good husband. Now we have a good marriage. How is that a lie?

Katherine

What if he remembers?

Elena

I'll cross that bridge when it collapses.

(then)

One day at a time, remember? Today I'm sober, I got a good marriage, my husband loves me, I got no complaints. Tomorrow I could be dead…Why borrow trouble today?

Katherine

I can't say she's wrong.

(then)

I'm supposed to lose weight because skinny is easier on the joints, but I know I could be dead tomorrow and I love chocolate cake. Do you think I'm going to eat carrots and celery?

Elena

One more thing. My sex life is now fantastic. That's all.

Rachel

Good for you!

(whispering to Cassie)

I told you I should bop Stan over the head. My sex life's so bad I'm practically a virgin again.

Cassie

(laughing at Rachel)

Terri?

Terri

(shyly)

I met a guy.

Katherine

(very alert)

Is he married?

Terri gives Katherine one of her "are you crazy" looks.

Terri

What would I want with an old, married dude? Yuck.

Katherine

(smiling)

Sorry. I was thinking of somebody else.

(then)

What's he like?

Terri

Lynnie introduced him to me. His name is Mike. He's an electrician. He did some work for the circus while they were here, but he mostly works for contractors in the Valley.

Rachel

(impressed)

He has a REAL job.

Terri

He's also an artist. On weekends he sells his paintings in Venice.

(enthused)

I love his art! He throws a layer of paint on a canvas, waits for it to dry, then globs another layer on top of it. Then he takes a hammer and whacks both layers of paint. It's very surreal.

Katherine

(concerned)

Uh…but he's still an electrician, isn't he?

Rachel

Katherine is worried that he's going to quit wiring and whack paint full time.

Terri

He wouldn't do that. He supports his two sisters.

(heartfelt)

His parents both died while he was in trade school. I know how that feels. Not having parents, I mean.

Cassie

Yes, you do.

(then)

Mike sounds like an interesting guy.

(then)

How does he feel about you being in AA?

Terri

He was surprised because I'm so young, but he thinks it's good. His mom was an alcoholic. He says he's not up for any more drunk nightmares.

(smiles)

So now I've got another reason to feel good about staying sober.

Cassie

That's a nice thought. Hopefully, none of us is up for any more drunk nightmares.

Katherine

One day at a time.

I glance at my watch.

Cassie

Time for the basket.

As we pass the basket, I'm thinking that an AA meeting is like a chapter in a book that never ends. No tidy solutions or rides off into the sunset. We go through big, important events in our lives and succeed or fail, but that's not the end. There's always another challenge to face just around the corner, ready or not.

Life is like that old story about painting with mice. Just when you have all the mice arranged in perfect order on the canvas of your life, the mice get up and start running around in different directions. Constant change is the human condition. Constant striving is part of the process. If we're alive, we're chasing the mice.

Unlike books, our lives have no ending, happy or grim, until the moment we close our eyes for the last time. As long as we're breathing, it's never too late to have hope. As long as we live, it's never too late, or too early, to start all over again. As long as our hearts beat, we'll need each other because none of us can live a meaningful life alone. Without the experience, strength, and hope we can give each other, each of us is an island floating off to nowhere.

As long as I live, my salvation of choice, Alcoholics Anonymous, will be there for me. Long, long after I'm gone, AA will continue to be there for anyone willing to try it.

Keep coming back.

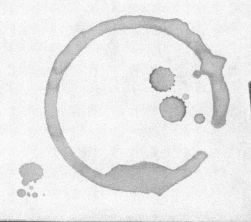

CHAPTER   TWENTY

For the sober members of many groups over the years

Thank you for being there when I walked in.

Thank you for taking me in.

Thank you for giving me the tools I needed to maintain my sobriety, the program, the Steps and most of all, for giving me your friendship.

Thank you for listening.

Thank you for your kindness when my heart was breaking over some personal issue.

Thank you for your toughness when I was feeling sorry for myself.

Thank you for allowing me to be a trusted servant even though I make awful coffee.

There are no words that can express the thanks I feel in my heart to every soul in AA I've met in the past and will meet in the future. You have saved my life and given me that "pearl of great price," sobriety. I am most humbly and forever in your debt.

Thank you.

Acknowledgements

An idea and enough time spent alone can result in a manuscript. But it's the encouragement, warmth and support of special friends and colleagues that helped carry me towards a finish line that so often seemed out of reach. Please know that your help and good wishes inform every page.

Nancy Cleary

Karen Kibler

Carol Summers

Ellen Bass

Kathy Good

Marcy Carsey

Barry Unger MD

James Rebeta

Carol Ann Rebeta

Mary Ann McKinnon

Matthew McKinnon

And, most importantly, my entire Family of Three Children, their Three Divine Spouses, Eight Grandchildren in assorted sexes and sizes and Six Great-Grandchildren including Triplets – for all the Joy you've given me there are no adequate words to express my profound gratitude. I Love You.

Each one of you has blessed my life in your own unique way. Thank you always.

CPSIA information can be obtained
at www.ICGtesting.com
Printed in the USA
FSHW011017180520
70338FS